THE FIFTH CATARACT

THE FIFTH CATARACT

Jo Bannister

This first world edition published in Great Britain 2005 by
SEVERN HOUSE PUBLISHERS LTD of
9–15 High Street, Sutton, Surrey SM1 1DF.
This first world edition published in the USA 2006 by
SEVERN HOUSE PUBLISHERS INC of
595 Madison Avenue, New York, N.Y. 10022.

British Library Cataloguing in Publication Data

Bannister, Jo
   The fifth cataract
   1.   Broads, The (England) - Fiction
   2.   Suspense fiction
   I.   Title
   823.9'14 [F]

   ISBN-10 : 0-7278-6284-7

Typeset by Palimpsest Book Production Ltd.,
Polmont, Stirlingshire, Scotland.
Printed and bound in Great Britain by
MPG Books Ltd., Bodmin, Cornwall.

I

First Impressions

One

B ad dreams stop when you wake up.

Otherwise, this had all the features of a nightmare. The surreal backdrop. The leprous half-light; the smell of sulphur. The damp, cloying cold, its chill fingers stroking the cringing body in alien, intimate ways. The crippling fear.

Most diagnostic of all, the absolute exhaustion. You can do hard physical labour until you drop and still not know that bone-crushing, mind-sapping exhaustion that visits you in your own bed in the middle of the night. You lie stiff, sweating in your hair, while forces you don't understand do battle over you and in you, and just before you wake you're aware of the absolute helplessness of being trapped in a body that's too tired to run and too weak to fight.

Then someone pokes you in the ribs and says, 'Stop whimpering,' or, 'You've woken me up *again*,' or, 'It's your turn to get breakfast; don't burn the toast,' and it's over. Bad as it was, it's over and not a shred of it – often not even the memory – remains to poison the day.

That's how I knew this wasn't a nightmare. However much I whimpered, Harry wasn't going to prod me in the ribs and tell me to get the coffee on. Harry was a hundred miles away; he wouldn't be getting up for an hour yet, and when he did he'd sip his coffee and wonder if I was having a good time.

He would not guess, and if I died here he would never know, that while he was burrowing under the duvet for those last precious minutes of sleep, I was fighting for my life – against the darkness, the cold, the grinding exhaustion and the black water that lurked beneath a scummy surface posing as solid ground. The first time I took that scum for grass I went in over my head and thought I'd drown. The second time I couldn't find a firm enough handhold to drag myself out and damn nearly *did* drown.

Almost, by then, I didn't care. For two pins I'd have stayed in the black pool until someone got round to hauling me out. Then I remembered who would find me and what that would be like. Desperation plumbed some well of strength I didn't know I had and I drove my fingers into the black mud and heaved myself out on my belly like a seal.

I would have given anything – soul, body or blood – for a chance to rest. To lie panting on the wet mud till the exhaustion cleared from my eyes and the pulse stopped pounding in my ears, till the circulation returned to the blocks of ice that hung heavy at the end of my legs where my feet used to be. But then I heard the sounds of pursuit: men's voices and feet splashing in the shallow pools.

They had come as far across this dark, dangerous wetland as I had, and they had come faster, but there was nothing to suggest that they felt how I felt. The voices were urgent, the steps quick and sure. And now the sulphurous light was growing. Soon they would see me, and soon after that they would catch me.

I had reached the end of my strength. I couldn't outrun them and I couldn't fight them off. One option remained. Leaden-hearted, I slid silently back into the black pool, lowering myself until only my nose broke the scummy surface. The stench rasped in my throat. The sounds of pursuit came to me like an echo, distorted by the water in my ears. I held my breath, and waited for triumph to lift the voices and hands to fasten in my clothes.

Instead they passed over me – literally, hurdling the pool I lay in – and didn't see me or suspect that I was there. The splashing feet ran on, the calling voices growing more querulous as they grew fainter.

Chilled as I was, I waited until they were almost out of earshot before I raised my head clear of the water to look for them. By then they were a quarter of a mile away, blending to grey and disappearing as the black fen swallowed up the first half-hearted gleam of daylight. They thought I was still ahead of them. I couldn't even manage a smile. I reached up the bank, clawing wearily in the mud, not sure I could clamber out again.

A strong hand gripped mine, and I breathed a little shriek and swallowed black water; then I was kneeling on the wet mud, nose to nose with my captor.

It was Costigian. Even in the half-light there was no mistaking the bear-like bulk of him. Hollis might have loomed as large but would have contrived it that the rising sun turned his blond hair to a halo. Also, he would have been crowing. This bear-like man crouching quietly beside me, as dirty as I was and maybe as tired, watching me half-humorously through a sodden fringe of thick brown hair, was Costigian.

I let go the last of my breath in a gusty sigh. 'I thought you'd be the one to give me trouble.'

He shrugged, the big shoulders hunched against the lightening sky. The transatlantic accent was musical in his low voice. 'I've done this for real. Knowing the guy up ahead's prepared to blow your head off concentrates the mind wonderfully.'

I was puzzled. 'There are still Indians in the Canadian bush?'

Costigian grinned. 'There are, but they don't let you shoot them any more.'

He might have been a soldier. But mostly he reminded me of Harry. 'Police?'

As if I'd said something tactless he looked away and didn't answer. I could have left it. It was none of my concern. But I'm bad at minding my own business. 'Your secret's safe with me. My husband's a policeman.'

'Yeah?' He stood up. 'Well I'm not.' He began to walk away. Away from me, away from the chase, away from the sun; back towards the land.

When I could get my feet under me I followed. 'Aren't you going to present me to Hollis and claim your reward?'

Costigian stopped and looked round, the amiable grin back on his broad face. 'An hour from now, when Hollis gives up looking and leads his weary band back to that toilet he calls Base Camp, and you and me are sitting there in dry clothes finishing a hot breakfast, the expression on his face is going to be all the reward I need.'

I couldn't think where I'd gone wrong. I thought I'd made myself perfectly clear. Working out the plot for my next book, I'd realized I needed to see a survival course in action. Though I consider myself a survivor, I'd never done it by numbers and I wanted to see how it worked.

There had never been any question of me joining in. I am not now, and never was even before I hit my mid-forties, of a physical persuasion. Like most novelists, I do on paper things I haven't the energy or the nerve to do for real. I lie for a living, all right? Nobody expected Agatha Christie to commit the murders she wrote about – why would you expect me to master the skills that spies and criminals depend on? I don't take part in car chases and I don't hurdle high hedges. At five-foot-two I have trouble *seeing* over high hedges. My typing fingers are the only bits of me that take regular exercise.

I had explained that to Tom Chase – very clearly, in words of one syllable – and I thought we had an understanding. When the senior partner in the Graveleigh School of Adventure assured me he saw no problems, I thought he meant there'd be no problem with me watching from the sidelines. What he actually meant was, there are no hedges in a salt marsh.

There were seven of us. Two of us were women. A plasterboard divider in the dormitory gave us a rudimentary privacy and we had our own washroom in a lean-to at our end, but that was where the conceit of separate facilities ended. In fact, that was where the facilities ended. Even the washrooms were an afterthought. Until last summer, said Chase, students were pointed towards the sea.

As the senior partner in the enterprise, it was Chase I'd spoken to on the phone. He and his colleague Terry Hollis had met us on the station at Spalding. Both of them were wearing T-shirts with the School of Adventure logo, but there the similarity ended. I guessed Chase was about my age. He wasn't a big man the way Costigian was big, but his spare body was toned and tough and he radiated a quiet determination that suggested he could go all day on a muesli bar, and then do it again tomorrow if he had to. I wasn't surprised to learn he'd done twelve years in the Parachute Regiment.

Hollis was fifteen years younger, four inches taller and three stone heavier than his partner. If this makes it to film, he'll be played by a middle-European body-builder with a bust size larger than his IQ. He looked beautiful on the brochure but he didn't inspire the sort of confidence that Chase did.

We had been warned not to bring cars because the track to Base Camp was often impassable. The Adventure School had a minibus mounted on the high doughnut wheels of an all-terrain vehicle. Chase and Hollis collected us from Spalding station at five o'clock in the afternoon on the last Saturday in August.

By then the rest of us had recognized one another by our air of wary anticipation and traded names and excuses. Mine was about the best: my work required it. A couple of people claimed to be here by choice, a couple more conceded an element of necessity. We were five men and two women, five adults and two teenagers, six Brits and a Canadian – seven people who should have got straight back on to the trains that disgorged us and never mind our lost deposits. But it was both too late and too soon to be thinking like that.

There was a certain amount of wry laughter, but the prevailing mood was of unease. Only one of us had done anything like this before and there was anxiety about how demanding it was going to be, whether they would prove equal to the challenge. I say *they* because I wasn't in the least bit anxious. I knew I was up to the challenge of taking notes.

But I was glad to find I wasn't the only woman there. Not out of concern for my virtue but because a group of men out to impress one another make tedious company. The same thought must have occurred to Marion Fletcher, because her eyes lit up when she saw me. 'Thank God. I've been scared this was going to be a testosterone-fest.'

7

She was twelve years younger and six inches taller than me, with bright green eyes and auburn hair cut rigorously short. She said she was a civil servant, that she was here because her job involved too much sitting at a desk to keep her physically fit. This had sounded more fun than joining a gym.

'Fun?' I asked, deadpan.

'Have you ever been to a gym?' she responded; and I had to admit that I hadn't.

As the people with homes and jobs to go to cleared the platform, other members of our merry band became apparent. Jimmy Ferris drifted over and introduced himself indistinctly through a wad of chewing-gum. He was about nineteen, with eyes the colour of washing-up water. I doubted he'd had a square meal or a good bath in the last month. He didn't volunteer a reason for his presence, but I thought I could guess: his father had wanted him out of the house for a week.

I'd bumped into Costigan on the train – literally: we'd been sidling past one another when the carriage lurched, throwing me against his shoulder. He caught his breath as if I'd hurt him. But before I could apologize he'd set me on my feet again and retreated behind an amiable grin, and we continued in our opposite directions.

Now we traded nods of recognition. 'Clio Marsh,' I said.

'Costigan.'

I frowned. 'That's a name?'

'It is in Canada.'

He'd been in Britain for twelve months, he said, and would soon be going home. When I asked what he was doing in an East Anglian fen he grinned lazily. He had a broad, good-natured, homespun face with thick brown hair falling just a shade longer than was fashionable over a wide brow. 'I'm out of shape. I've been away too long. If I go back like this I'm going to get laughed at.'

Maybe, by a grizzly bear out to impress its friends – no one else. Besides, it wasn't true. On his big frame it would have showed if he'd been running to fat. All he was carrying was a healthy covering for a man in his mid-thirties who was never going to be a professional athlete now.

Perhaps that was the problem. Around thirty-five a man can start worrying about all the things he didn't do while he was wasting his youth on fast girls and cheap cars. Middle age is only a heartbeat away and it suddenly strikes him that this is his last chance, that anything he needs his prime for he'd better do soon. So men who haven't walked anywhere since they got their first clapped-out Mini start jogging, and men who thought *going for the burn* meant trout-fishing put themselves on the rack of circuit training. Lots of them end up in doctors' surgeries.

But Costigian wasn't the type to be panicked into desperate measures – and I didn't yet know how desperate a measure this was – because his Levis would only fasten if he stopped breathing. He was fit enough, and I thought he'd seen enough of the world to know that. So he had something else in mind.

But before I could find out what, another train paused long enough on the platform to disgorge, among the women loaded down with toddlers and shopping, another trio of survivalists: two men and a boy.

George Fox came handshake first. He was taller than Costigian and rangy, with long bones, sandy hair and frank, cheerful eyes. He was about thirty. John Tarrant was a few years younger, inches shorter, compact, quiet and self-contained. And Nick Baker might have been seventeen with a following wind, wearing a hand-knitted sweater that I guessed was the price for being allowed to come. When he phoned home tonight it would be the first thing his mother would ask: 'Are you wearing your jumper?' And he'd answer yes, but actually, when he saw the rest of us in T-shirts, he quickly shrugged it off and stuffed it into his pack.

But there was no time for us to trade histories with these last arrivals because by then the management were checking us off on their clipboard. We answered to our names. All present and correct, they herded us towards their high-stepping minibus. A steel ladder folded down at the rear. A discreet shove from Costigian got me up it and I thought, Ho ho, it's a good job nobody's expecting *me* to do anything energetic. The others followed and the instructors climbed

9

up in front and slammed the doors. By then it was too late for second thoughts. We were committed.

And still most of us were thinking of it as a holiday.

No one more than George. He was the one who'd done this before – several times, actually, not at Graveleigh but at other locations in Britain and abroad. He'd done the first for a bet and the others because he enjoyed the experience. He was a long-distance lorry-driver, a job which like Marion's – like mine – involved a lot of sitting in one place. He found this the perfect antidote.

As he talked – easily and unselfconsciously, a natural communicator – I felt the anxiety quotient in the back of the bus start to reduce. Of course, George wasn't the perfect template for our group – he was younger than some of us and fitter than most – but it was reassuring to meet someone who had good reason to think we might enjoy this.

Nick too was optimistic about the week ahead, but not because he had any idea what to expect. He'd won his place as a school prize, but not for anything that might have come in useful – athletics, for instance, or rugby. He was head of the Debating Society.

John wasn't here to enjoy himself. He was here to work, and he had a goal to work towards. In the course of an hour's drive, with the roads deteriorating first to lanes, then to tracks, finally to mere marks in the mud, we got his story out of him. All right, *I* got his story out of him. That's what I was there for: to learn about survival and survivalists, their drives and motivations – what made them put themselves through the wringer when they could have gone to Alicante instead.

For John the answer was, his life's ambition. Since someone gave him a toy rifle for his sixth birthday he'd wanted to be a soldier. He'd eaten, slept and dreamed the Army. At six it was kind of cute, at twelve already a little childish, at fifteen downright perverse. But when he'd turned eighteen and still wanted to be a soldier his parents, free-loving hippies in their own youth, had resigned themselves to having raised a throwback and set about helping him.

He was the sort of material recruiting sergeants would die

for: polite, intelligent, motivated, a young man who desperately wanted to be a career soldier. All his assessments were good, but he couldn't make the grade physically. He wasn't soft, he just hadn't the strongest physique in the world. Twice he got halfway through basic training and had to retire injured.

Most people would have taken the hint, but this was what John had wanted to do since he was a child. Before he had one last shot at it he meant to spend three months on concentrated physical training. Graveleigh was part of his campaign. If after that he still wasn't tough enough he would look for something else to do with his life. But the knowledge that it would be second best was already there in his eyes. He'd break himself in pieces before he'd admit defeat this time.

There was a moment's quiet in the bus when he finished, because most of us had at some time wanted something we couldn't have, and we wished him well even though experience suggested he was beating his head on a brick wall.

Jimmy Ferris had never had an ambition to be thwarted in. He wasn't trying to be the first kid on his block with a Porsche. He'd have liked to be the first with a criminal record, but even that accolade had gone to someone who was prepared to work for it. Jimmy's forte was sneering at better men. 'You wouldn't catch me in the bleeding Army. Poncing around with bleeding guns and stuff. Bleeding marching and stuff.'

Which is when Tom Chase told us he'd been in the Falklands War, crossing the island on foot to take part in the battle for Stanley. And that it had involved marching, and guns, and also bleeding.

Into the silence that followed Marion Fletcher said pointedly, 'So, not a bit like what you're doing now?'

And we all laughed, and thought it was a joke.

11

Two

The wind came out of the east, off the North Sea, smelling of salt and distance. The last land it had seen had been the Frisian Islands. Neither high enough nor hard enough to impede its progress, their only contribution had been to act as a whetstone to a knife. Honed to a cold hard sharpness that made no concession to the season, it soughed up the beach and over the salt flats, flaying the skin from my face and the hands I put up to protect it. Oh yes: it was raining too.

The last living soul to have felt that wind was a Texel sheep, and it had the sense to wear wool. I was wearing a rather chic little tracksuit I'd picked up in a Skipley boutique.

It was nobody's fault but my own. If I'd signed up for a week's sailing I'd have dressed in oiled-wool sweaters and Norwegian socks, pulled waterproofs over the top and finished the ensemble with a bright-yellow sou'wester. I'd have looked like an extra from *The Pirates of Penzance*, but I'd have been warm.

I'd seen the brochures of sunny Norfolk beaches, and certainly sailing the Broads is a different thing from sailing the open sea; and while I'd realized this wasn't going to be a beach holiday, I'd expected the same sort of weather as they get at Cromer.

My fundamental mistake was in thinking of the marsh as land. It isn't: neither land nor sea, too thick to drink and too thin to plough. What lies behind the protective reef of salt-ings and mudbanks appears on maps as part of England rather than the North Sea, but it's land heavily diluted by sea water, not so much a shore as an expanse of seabed hauled up just above high-water mark.

So the wind racing over it was a sea wind, the chill rising off it the chill of fathoms, and my trendy tracksuit didn't begin to meet my needs here. I wasn't sure which stung most: the cold, or making a fool of myself.

Young Nick came to the rescue. He'd seen me shiver, and when we went back indoors I found his hand-knitted sweater lying on my bed. It was a bit long for me, but I turned up the sleeves till my fingertips showed and pulled the hem down over my thighs, and began to feel human again. At the supper table I leaned forward over the baked beans and kissed him soundly, and a pleased flush spread up his scrubbed young face.

In other ways supper was less of a success. Not only the food, which was as primitive and nasty as we'd every reason to expect, but – from my perspective much worse, though it seemed to afford my companions a degree of cheap merriment – the discovery that Chase had misunderstood my request. He seemed to think I had come not to watch but to take part.

I referred him to our correspondence of a month before. 'You said you saw no problem.'

He smiled, untroubled. 'We seem to have been at cross-purposes. I meant I saw no problem about you doing one of our courses. Look, we're all at different levels of fitness. Every course we run has to cater for people with different strengths and abilities. Some of our students spend all year behind a desk – they come here precisely because it's so different. It's a learning process, not an endurance test.'

'But – but . . .' I heard myself stammering and stopped. 'I'm forty-five years old!'

'I'm forty-seven.'

'I'm only five-foot-two!'

Sensing blood, Hollis joined in. 'One of the best students we ever had here was a girl gymnast. Four-foot-eleven in her hiking boots.'

'I needed help getting on the sodding bus!'

'Then that can be your target for the week,' Chase said briskly. 'Not leaving here as a paratrooper, but being able to get on the bus unaided. Tell you what: tomorrow morning we'll be up before dawn for a stroll across the marsh. So you won't have trouble keeping up, we'll give you a head start . . .'

Which is how I came to be playing hare to a pack of hounds on average twenty years younger and eight inches taller than me, at an hour I hadn't seen in a very long time, over a landscape indistinguishable from chocolate mousse except by the taste.

Before we'd left Base Camp, Chase had given us a lecture. 'Survival isn't something you do on your own, at least not for long. Sooner or later – and in the conditions you'll meet out there it'll be sooner – you'll find you need other people. You'll start acting as a group. You'll identify your own strengths and weaknesses, and those of everyone round you. It's a gradual process; it might take most of the week, but when you leave here you'll know what it feels like to be part of a team.

'That's a legacy you'll carry for the rest of your lives. You may meet in pubs to throw darts at pictures of me and Terry, or you may never see one another again. But the idea of taking responsibility for other people will stay with you. You'll be better, stronger people for it.'

They gave me fifteen minutes and the whole of the marsh to lose myself in. Before he started the clock Chase reminded me that this was a dangerous environment and should be treated with respect. 'You'll never be out of earshot. If you get into trouble, keep still and shout. If you think you're sinking, lie flat. We'll be with you in a couple of minutes.'

Sweetening the pot was Hollis's idea. 'I've got some cigars in my locker. Whoever runs her down wins one.'

'I don't smoke cigars,' Marion said pointedly.

Hollis made no attempt to disguise his scorn. 'We'll cross that bridge if we come to it.'

I sniffed. 'What if nobody catches me?'

'In that case,' said Hollis with a handsome, confident smile that I wanted to hit with a brick, 'you get to choose. Either you smoke the cigar, or I'll eat it.'

When Costigian and I got back to Base Camp there was no one else there. We lit the stove and changed out of the fluorescent jumpsuits provided for use in the marsh and into dry

14

clothes. Still struggling into his sweater he said, 'I've been caught in cloudbursts warmer than that shower.'

'They're trying to toughen us up.'

'Well, I've seized up.' When I tried to help, he grunted. I remembered bumping into him on the train and his grimace then.

I said, 'Sore shoulder? Let me help, I'm a doctor.'

'Are you?' Of course, I'd told them I was a writer.

'I haven't practised for a while. But I think I can remember what to do for fibrositis.' I pushed his shirt up at the back. When I saw what the problem was I stopped dead.

'It isn't fibrositis,' he said.

It was a gunshot wound – months old and well healed, but unmistakably the result of hot lead entering his body at high velocity.

I waited until I was sure something would come out when I opened my mouth. 'That time when you did this for real. You didn't do it too well, did you?'

He'd finally got his arm into his sleeve. Now he pulled his clothes down over the scar – not angrily but quietly, watching for a reaction. 'I did it great,' he said, his low voice with its faint burr of an accent gentle and even humorous. 'Every time except the last one.'

But I was – I don't know: alarmed? Angry? I'm not sure why. Perhaps because I hate surprises. 'How did you come by that?'

'None of your business,' he said calmly, tucking his shirt in. 'You ready for your breakfast?' He lifted the pan off the heat.

I took it off him and slammed it back on the stove. 'Damn breakfast. Costigian, you heard the induction lecture. That's not an adventure playground out there. There's a real risk of people getting lost, or hurt, or worse. We're going to depend for our safety on one another. That *makes* it my business. Anyone on this course could find his life in your hands and we need to know if we can rely on you. Or if you're some kind of a hood.'

He went on looking at me as he had throughout this start-led tirade, amiable and faintly amused. Perhaps he wasn't

15

used to being shouted at by people who didn't block his view. Then he picked up the frying pan again and helped himself. 'I'm not a hood.'

I couldn't make him tell me who had shot him and why. But I didn't understand why, if it was nothing to be ashamed of, he wouldn't explain. Merely because I had no right to ask? Either way, my options were limited. I could tell Chase. There was nothing else I could do.

Soon afterwards we heard footsteps heavy on the boards outside and the door opened.

You never saw seven such sorry-looking specimens in all your life. They were mud from top to toe – so much so that I had trouble knowing which was Marion.

'OK,' said Tom Chase, dripping cheerfully towards the men's washroom, 'showers first, then breakfast, then the inquest.'

I felt hostility rake the back of my neck as Hollis passed behind me. Costigian's eyes were on my face. If I was going to give him away, now was the time.

I said over my shoulder, 'Don't forget the cigar.'

It lay on the table between us while we ate. Costigian made no attempt to claim it, and certainly I didn't. When all that was left was the coffee, Chase said, 'What happened?'

I was going to tell him, but Costigian got in first. 'I'd had enough so I dropped out and came back. Clio was here when I arrived.'

I stared at him. The brown eyes were unconcerned.

'Clio?'

'Er . . .' I minced along the tightrope between making myself a liar and calling Costigian one. 'I hid in one of the pools. You ran over the top of me.'

Hollis snarled, 'We've been searching that bloody marsh for an hour! We thought you'd drowned. Someone could have been hurt while you were in here with your feet up!'

I started to apologize but again Costigian interrupted. 'Looking after you was no part of her brief. Her job was giving you the slip, and she did it.'

Chase nodded. 'I said there was more than one way of doing this. All the same, we'll have to be more careful in

16

future. I don't want people wandering around aimlessly – that's how accidents happen. My fault: if I'd sent George, say, I'd have told him how to signal the game was over. I underestimated you, Clio. I won't make that mistake again.' A quirk of humour at the corner of his mouth took the edge off what might have been a threat.

Everyone was looking at the cigar. Nick, who had recovered his bounce with the natural resilience of a fed teenager, picked it up and offered it to me. 'Are you going to smoke it?'

I shuddered. 'I'd rather face the marsh again.'

Nick reached for the tomato ketchup, squeezed a careful trickle down the length of the cigar and put it in front of Hollis. And we all watched with interest to see what he would do.

What he did was remember.

We stood at the bottom of the wall looking up. Then we looked at one another. Then we looked at Hollis, who smirked. Then we looked at Chase doling out crash-hats. Then, almost in unison, we shook our heads and began to get back in the bus.

Tom Chase chuckled. 'It's not as bad as it looks. There are plenty of holds. Remember, you'll be on a rope.'

Not Hollis, though. Hollis climbed free with the coiled rope slung over one shoulder: if he made a mistake as he reached the top he had fifteen metres in free fall. And this was no custom-built climbing wall, it was the gable end of a house – a soaring edifice of ashlar blocks raised in tribute to his own importance by the Victorian landowner when Graveleigh had enjoyed a modest prosperity as a grain-growing area, before the tidal surge of March 1883 breached the dune-line and inundated the fields behind. Now it was impossible to judge which was virgin marsh and which drowned farmland, and even the house had broken before the might of the storm. All that stood now was the gable end and one corner.

I hadn't thought much of Hollis until then. He'd struck me as being all mouth and chest-expanders. But watching him go up that wall my admiration soared. He probably

17

climbed it once a week all summer long, but you're never so good at something that you can't make a mistake, and a mistake up there would have broken his powerful young body into a million pieces.

You wouldn't have known it to watch him. His confidence, so irritating at ground level, was a joy to behold as his strong muscles powered him upwards, long limbs stretching for the holds. He climbed without haste or hesitation, and almost before I felt the need to breathe again had reached the top and roped himself on. When he turned and grinned down at us, the sense of achievement was positively engaging. I thought I would try to like him a little more.

George went next. Lacking Hollis's familiarity with the wall, he took longer and tested his holds more carefully. But he was plainly another climber. The rope, which Hollis shortened as George went higher, was never taut between them and in a few minutes he threw a long leg over the gable as casually as mounting a bar stool.

Quick as he'd gone up, he came down quicker, leaping off the wall backwards into space. His boots made a graceful parabola against the sky, kicking off the masonry at measured intervals until he landed beside me.

Costigian too was familiar with the technique. The weakness of his right arm was a problem: he compensated by choosing a different route up the wall. Still there were times when all he could do was hang on grimly, most of his weight on that damaged shoulder and his face locked tight against the pain. Only sheer bloody-minded refusal to admit defeat got him to the top.

Abseiling down, at least he had gravity on his side. He accepted our congratulations, and when John began to climb moved away unnoticed.

I went after him. No one missed me, and Costigian didn't know I was there until I said softly, 'Bad?'

His face was grey, the muscles cording along his jaw. 'Yeah.'

'Let me help.' Even through the sweater I could feel the muscles knotted round the injury in a hard slab. He grunted down his nose as I probed with my fingertips.

He had two options. One was to retire to a hot bath and stop trying to force his body to be as strong as it had been before he was shot. The other was to work through it, break up that angry knot in his back and make the muscles get on with their job. I knew what I'd have done, and also what I'd have advised if he'd been my patient. 'Are you planning to go on with this?'

'Oh yes.' There was pain in his voice but no doubt.

'It's going to hurt.'

'It hurts now.'

'More than that.'

'Don't talk,' he said. 'Do it.'

So while the second division tackled the wall with varying degrees of effectiveness and elan, I was kneading my thumbs deep into the raging muscles of Costigian's right shoulder, feeling his back arch with the pain, hearing the sounds in his throat that he couldn't quite swallow. And knowing that I shouldn't be doing this. I wasn't effecting a cure, I was just making it possible for him to go on subjecting himself to strains he wasn't capable of absorbing. What if I made it possible for him to climb that wall again and couldn't do a thing to save him from falling off?

I stopped abruptly. 'This is crazy. Nothing that hurts this much can possibly be doing you any good.'

'I'm OK.' He had enough mobility now to look round and smile at me. His colour was coming back and the rigid lines of his face had softened. 'I promise, I'm not going to do myself any lasting harm. But time's a factor here, and I can take a bit of hurting if it'll speed things up. I need to get back to work, and I can't spend another six months recuperating.'

I was going to ask him what was so urgent that it was worth not only this amount of pain but that amount of risk. But then Chase called my name, and when I looked round he had the end of the rope in his hand.

Everyone was very kind. No one laughed, the subject was quickly changed, and several of them mentioned, casually, as if they'd just remembered, how I'd made fools of them on the marsh. Even Hollis was matter-of-fact about it. 'Some people just can't deal with heights.'

I'd panicked. I got to a point where all the obvious holds were out of reach, and instead of climbing down a little and trying another route I lunged for a grip that I could barely touch, and I fell. Only half a metre, until Hollis caught me on the rope. I wasn't hurt and I'd never been in danger. But I couldn't find the nerve to go on climbing.

I tried a couple of times, wedged my fingers into good deep cracks and my toes into firm little ledges, gritted my teeth and tried to continue. I knew that if I could make the top, however much help I needed, everyone there would count it a success. But I no longer believed it was possible. I began to shake, and for long minutes couldn't even find my way down again.

At the bottom my companions were too busy retying bootlaces and blowing noses to meet my eyes. I wished someone would laugh and make a joke of it. A heat rose up my body until it blazed in my cheeks.

Chase said calmly, 'It's *supposed* to be difficult. If it was easy, anyone could do it.' But Hollis had done it without a rope, and Costigian had done it with an injured shoulder, and everyone else had done it one way or another. 'If there's time later in the week, and if you want to, we'll come back and have another go.' And I was appalled at the very idea.

In the afternoon we went canoeing. There were five kayaks pulled up on the mud where a river disgorged into the great cold-water bay of the Wash, so we divided into two groups. I think Chase was making it easy for me when he put me with Marion and Nick, but his concern was misplaced. Boats I can do. I paddled rings round the others, did Eskimo rolls and emergency exits, and felt a glimmer of self-worth returning.

Then we surrendered the canoes to the second group. I got Jimmy into mine. He looked terribly unstable, shocked at the way his body was swinging. It's like riding a bicycle: you stay upright mainly by believing that you can. Jimmy believed he'd turn over so in due course he did. There was a nasty moment before he kicked himself free, but Hollis wasn't far away on one side and Costigian was closer on the other, and they had him back in the canoe before he had the chance to refuse. Costigian stayed beside him while he learnt the feel of the frail craft.

Beside me Marion gave a disparaging sniff. We'd found a little shelter from the wind beneath the river bank. 'Look at that,' she said sourly, 'Eskimo Nell.'

She was watching Costigian. And it occurred to me that I'd seen her watching him before. A little holiday romance would cheer the place up, but Costigian? I didn't know how good an idea that was. I had too many questions about Costigian.

I needn't have worried. It wasn't lust in her eyes but irritation. 'Look at that big moose showing off. OK, we know, you've played out in canoes before.'

'Goes with the territory, I suppose,' I said mildly. 'A Canadian who couldn't paddle a canoe would be like a Mountie who couldn't ride a horse.'

Marion glared at me from under her brows. 'And *that*'s an overrated establishment too,' she muttered darkly. At the time I had no idea what she meant.

Where the peat-brown water of the river met the mud-brown shallows of the sea, Nick was prancing through knee-high spume and shouting advice to Jimmy. He fancied his chances with a canoe. He had tried, not once but several times, to match my roll. He never made it all the way round but that didn't stop him trying. It didn't stop him telling Jimmy how to do it, either, though Jimmy was only interested in staying upright.

Finally Jimmy could endure the younger boy's taunts no longer. He ran his canoe up the beach, struggled out and hurled himself at Nick with threats, vile language and shrieks of laughter. Helpless with mirth, they fell about in the mud, covering themselves from head to foot. They slipped and slithered, pushed one anothers' faces in it, slid down it into the river like a pair of young otters.

Marion was still watching the canoeists with a jaundiced eye, her lips moving in silent curses. When I concentrated I could make out the words: 'Fall in. Fall in.'

Three

After supper Chase and Hollis retired to their office to write up their notes ('Clio Marsh: too old, too short, too soft; could do better, probably won't'). Marion and I were sprawled on our bunks recovering from the day's exertions when there was a tap on the partition and Costigian's head appeared. 'We're going to the pub. Are you coming?'

'Pub?' We said it in unison, like a choral-speaking duet, with the same upward inflection of amazed disbelief. Here? In the middle of the chocolate mousse?

One ear cocked towards the office, he waved us to secrecy. 'We don't have a pass. We're going over the wall.'

Marion and I had already decided on an early night. We thought of warm duvets cosseting aching limbs and sleep drawing a blessed curtain on the day. Then we thought of a week without alcohol, of being constantly wet and totally dry. 'We'll see you outside in five minutes,' said Marion.

Neither of us had brought any going-out clothes. We pulled on the things we had travelled in, which were the most respectable we had, and trainers – almost dry after an hour grouped round the stove – because after the day they'd had our feet would have rebelled at shoes. Then, feeling about fourteen years old, we sneaked outside.

The escape committee consisted of us three and George Fox. John was studying and the boys didn't relish a cosy evening in a country pub. Costigian told them we'd be back before midnight, that if anyone wanted us we'd be at The Wake in Graveleigh.

I hadn't realized there was a village. But the man who had built the big house wouldn't have done his own ploughing or taken his harvest away in a rowing boat. Then more than

22

now, any kind of trade here required a harbour, and a harbour meant a village.

It was a mile across the marsh from Base Camp. It would have been closer as the crow flies, but that way a fish could swim too. It might have been worth trying in full daylight in our fluorescent suits, but even if we arrived safely in the gathering dusk we wouldn't be allowed in. So we stuck to the road. At least the rain eased off as we were leaving.

As we walked we wondered how Costigian had known the pub was there – he insisted that, just as some people can dowse for water, he had an instinct for the nearest beer – and why it was called The Wake. I reckoned it was because fishermen homeward-bound on a Friday night left a sign-post in the sea behind them. George said it was named for Hereward the Wake, the Saxon outlaw whose rebellion against William the Conqueror had been based a little south of here at Ely. But when we got there we found that Marion had been right: she'd said it was the sort of place where people joined hands and tried to get in touch with the living.

It wasn't just the pub: Graveleigh was the same. It was like a ghost town or a stage set; or like finding yourself shrunk down and planted in a model village, architecturally perfect and quite dead.

The walk from Base Camp took twenty minutes and served to loosen stiff muscles and relax tired minds. By the time we had the village in sight we were all feeling fresher, the mood lighter. We discussed the day, at first like mature adults analysing their performance, then like third-formers giggling over what they'd said to teacher.

Because the marsh was flat, the road across it flat and the village built where the flatness of the land met the flatness of the sea, there was no question of topping a rise and finding ourselves in the main street. Graveleigh grew imperceptibly, almost organically, out of the evening with every step we took. From the moment our track joined the causeway across the marsh and we turned towards the sea, we could see the broken line of roofs. As the evening advanced, a few lights sprang up. They made the place look even further away, receding from us as we approached as if in a bad dream,

23

which arriving did nothing to dispel. The buildings were real – single-storey cottages mostly in flint, two-storey ones rendered in pastel shades that had long since faded to grey – but somehow the idea of a village had gone on receding. All that remained was a shell.

I know I have an overactive imagination. It goes with the job. But from the way my companions broke step and hesitated, looking about them in puzzlement, they too felt like intruders in a cemetery. There were no people. There were a couple of dozen cottages, huddled under low roofs, backing on to the little stone harbour where a single trawler and a few smaller boats were tied to the wall. We passed a closed shop and a tiny bricked-up schoolhouse. But there were no people. No one in the street, no one at the harbour, no one that we could see at the windows.

Marion muttered, 'I think the bomb's dropped and nobody's told us.'

George shook his sandy head decisively. 'Plague. Any second now an old man wrapped in rags will stagger down the street, ringing a bell and howling, "Unclean, unclean."' Marion glared at him and he chuckled. But the image lingered on the evening air like the smell of rain.

Costigian was not an imaginative man. 'Found it,' he said with satisfaction, wheeling right down an alley to a heavy door under a hanging sign.

The Wake had started life, long before the big house, as a single-storey flint cottage. An upper storey had been added to accommodate travellers when the harbour was built. But the half-century while the cornfields of Graveleigh were pouring a steady golden stream into the holds of fat-bellied little traders for shipping to the new industrial cities were the only boom years the place had ever seen. Even Victorian industry was no match for the might of the sea, and when it had co-operated long enough, with one great storm it drowned the land and reclaimed the marsh. The sea gave Graveleigh its brief prosperity, and the sea took it away.

Our first impression as we came in off the street was that the Wake hadn't seen a customer since. It wasn't true, of course: there was one there now, propped up in the corner, hunched over a glass. He looked as if he might have ducked inside to avoid the 1883 inundation and never got round to leaving. One of these days the publican would try to give him a refill and find he'd been dead for weeks.

Because there was a publican too, and at first sight he too appeared to have been a left-over Victorian. He was short and thickset, and his eyes peered sharply from between his thick black hair and heavy beard like a water-rat peeping out of a river bank. But if he was excited to see four customers at once he showed no signs of it. He waited as long as he could without forcing us to complain, then heaved himself round to face us, leaning heavily on his elbows on the bar, and said, 'Yes?' as if afraid we might read some welcome into it.

George nodded brightly and said, 'Yes, thank you,' and went on standing there expectantly.

As if it was costing him blood the publican said, 'What do you want to drink?' He was a younger man than I had supposed, early twenties maybe, and his sharp light tenor voice was not what you expected coming from that jungle of beard. Looking again I realized he had grown the beard for a purpose. There was something wrong with his face.

There was a table near the window. George gave our orders then steered us towards it. He told the barman, 'Bring them over when they're ready,' and sat with his back to the bar so his eye couldn't be caught.

The Wake was about as conducive to cheery banter as a funeral parlour, but we made an effort. I was still trying to work Costigian out. 'Tell us about Canada.'

His face lit up with obvious affection. 'How long have you got? Canada's too big to sum up in three sentences.'

'Of course it is,' said Marion roughly. 'Too high and too wide and far too bloody thick.'

Costigian ignored her and began to describe the place where he was born. It sounded like Graveleigh with polar bears. Visitors had a choice of postcards to send home: either 'The Fishing Fleet', five old sea-buckets rusting picturesquely behind a net full of seal-sized holes, or 'The Traffic Lights, Main Street'.

We laughed – except for Marion – but Costigian didn't care. He shrugged happily, content with his memories. Then he looked past us and his grin died, leaving his broad face still. 'George . . .'

It was our drinks arriving. The boy with the beard had brought them as he'd been told, but God knows how. He was about as crippled as you can be outside a wheelchair, his back twisted, his legs hopelessly bent. He had a crutch wedged under each armpit and I don't know how he carried a tray. Under the beard his face was twisted too, partly with the disfigurement but mainly with sheer helpless fury at how he'd been humiliated – not even so much by George as by life.

George got up so quickly he knocked his chair over and took the tray. He said probably the only thing capable of injecting a little dignity into the moment. 'I'm sorry.'

He paid for the drinks. 'Will you join us?'

Some of the impotent rage had gone from the boy's face but not enough for him to want our company. 'No. Thanks.'

The conversation was rather muted after that. We talked about the weather, the endless unseasonable rain, and how many different ways we could get wet tomorrow; and the men drank with a kind of dedication as if it were a race. I thought they were eager to leave. But when Costigian finished and went to get up, George waved him back. 'Let me.' The Canadian nodded.

'Same again?' George went to the bar and waited for the drinks, and he brought ours over but returned to sip his at the bar. After a moment the boy relented and poured himself one too. Bizarrely enough, I saw him look at George's trainers first.

'Clio,' George called a minute later, 'you'll be interested in this. Saul's people have been here for generations; he knows everything there is to know about the marsh.' So I picked up my glass and went to join them. George introduced us: 'Clio Marsh, Saul Penny.' A moment later Marion and Costigian came over too, and we continued the evening ranged along the bar like locals.

Young Penny really did know everything about the area

26

and its history. He talked about the great inundation as if it had been the winter before last, and Squire Cottishall who had built the big house as if he might drop in for a hot toddy before closing time.

'It wasn't always called Graveleigh. The Squire called it Grainlee – for the harbour and the corn. Before that it didn't really have a name. On old maps, if it's there at all it's called The Island.' Ten minutes before, Saul Penny would have put his hand in the fire rather than talk to us. Now he was talking as fast as he could get the words out, as if someone might shut him up.

'Was it an island?' asked Marion.

'Not really.' Saul shook the black hair out of his eyes. 'I mean, it was always attached to the land. But for centuries the marsh was harder to cross than the sea. The track still washes out for days at a time. Last time we had to bring supplies in by boat was three winters back.'

I said, 'How many people live here now?'

He made a quick, dismissive shrug with shoulders massive from carrying his weight. 'A couple of dozen, just.'

'Where do they work?'

In the shadow of his beard his lip curled. 'Most of the people here are too old to work. There's a couple of boats still fishing, but they're doing well if they clear the cost of the diesel.'

In all probability there had been a community on The Island, taking a living from the sea, for a thousand years. No one had ever got rich here; some of them had starved; but they'd managed to raise children and pass something on from one generation to the next down all those centuries. The marsh had not beaten them. Even the sea had failed to dislodge them from their precarious foothold.

They had finally been beaten by public transport and the easier life waiting in the towns beyond the marsh. The young people had left Graveleigh in pursuit of the good life – all except Saul. When the old man in the corner and all the other old men and women in the old flint houses had died, when the fishing boats had tied up for the last time, there would be nothing left of Graveleigh but stones. The affluent society had achieved what a millennium of storms had not.

'Is there no employment locally?' asked George.

'There's the plant.' Saul's lip curled round the words as if on obscenities. 'I thought that was where you'd come from till I saw your shoes.'

We all looked at George's trainers. Unenlightened, we looked back at Saul. 'Plant?'

'Growth Industries. They make fertilizer and things.'

I didn't understand his hostility. A chemical plant should have provided jobs enough to keep people in Graveleigh. But it hadn't worked that way. Twenty-five years ago when the plant had opened, before Saul was born, there had been young men and women in the village to take employment there. But not enough, so workers had been brought in from outside as well. In time locals had married in-comers and left the Island. Only the old remained. Growth Industries had put the seal on Graveleigh's long decline.

George was looking for a silver lining. 'You must get good business from the plant. You're the only pub for miles.'

Again that bitter toss of the maned head. 'They don't come here. They wouldn't be welcome if they did.'

Perhaps it was natural to resent the industry which, with the best of intentions, had reduced his village to a ghost town. But his hostility denied him the benefits of a steady trade from the area's only mass employer. He had been ready to freeze us out until the sight of George's trainers persuaded him we were refugees from the survival school.

A door behind the bar opened and a man came through from the back room. Saul turned towards him with a curious ambivalence in what showed of his expression.

'Your mother's fine, Saul. She got a bit tired, that's all. I've left her some more of those pills; they seem to help.' He smiled. 'She says she could murder a cup of tea.'

'I'll go see to her.' Before he lurched away inside he poured Scotch into a tumbler and left it on the bar. 'Have a drink before you go. These people are from the survival school. They want to know why your plant coming here wasn't the best thing ever to happen to Graveleigh.'

The doctor watched him go, the smile still hovering about

28

his lips. He was an Edinburgh man. He might have been around forty, but he was the sort of medium-height, medium-build, intelligent-eyed scholarly man who wouldn't really show his age until the well-cut brown hair started thinning. He introduced himself as Donald Rodway and we offered our names in return.

I asked how long he'd worked at the plant, and whether his practice extended to Graveleigh.

'A couple of months, just,' he said. 'And no, not officially. But if anybody here needs a doctor, it's me or it's someone ten miles away across the marsh. So it tends to be me. My bosses are happy to do something for the village.'

'In spite of which they don't seem to be flavour of the month,' I said, and Rodway gave a rueful chuckle.

'Saul has his own opinions. He has a point, but after all these years he's about the only one keeping the feud going. Graveleigh was declining when the plant opened. Maybe it hastened the process, maybe not, but there's nothing to be done about it now. It's foolish to keep piling coals on a grievance a quarter of a century old.'

'Feeling as he does, I'm surprised he doesn't make his GP drive the ten miles to see his mother.'

Rodway shrugged. 'Apparently my predecessor knew her from when she worked at GI, years ago. Saul wouldn't admit it but he's glad to have me near. Mrs Penny's not in great health.' He sipped his Scotch reflectively.

'He might be a bit more gracious about it, then.'

'Well, Saul blames GI for the way he is. His mother was working at the plant's canteen when she was carrying him. He thinks the chemicals did something to her that made her an invalid and him a cripple. It's nonsense of course; that's what health and safety laws are for, but he won't be told. He'll die thinking Growth Industries ruined his life.'

Four

The next day it was raining again. Cold as sleet, it poured endlessly out of the low grey overcast. The ceaseless wind put a slant of forty-five degrees on it and drove it against the windows of Base Camp like gunfire. The windows began to leak. Every time someone opened a door a gust of rainstorm bellied in.

The marsh danced with it. The idea of dry land, always a dangerous illusion in a bog, became a farce. There *was* no land: its place had been taken by an inconvenient kind of water just too solid to sail over.

We had smelled it growing closer again as we walked back from the pub the previous night. The first thin drops caught us as we hurried down the track to Base Camp. If Dr Rodway hadn't dropped us at the junction on his way back to Growth Industries we'd have been drenched. But we thought there was time for it to clear before morning.

Rain in the fens doesn't work that way. Once it builds up a good head of cloud, brown and grey like the marsh beneath, it opens like emptying a bath, and it can keep it up for a week.

I nodded at the window as we were having breakfast. 'Pity about that,' I said, not altogether sincerely. 'What do you do here when it rains?'

'Same as we do when it doesn't,' Hollis said grimly, shovelling beans.

It wasn't just the weather that made breakfast a gloomy affair. There was ill-feeling about the night before. Not just our expedition to the pub but what had happened after we left. Midway through the evening, seeing the rain had stopped, the boys had gone out for a game of hide-and-seek in the marsh.

Jimmy hid and Nick sought. There was much splashing around and muffled giggling. But when Nick finally found Jimmy they had both lost Base Camp. It was going dark, the wind swallowed up their voices, and by the time they realized the hut wasn't where they thought they'd wandered a long way in the wrong direction.

They weren't afraid. They were two grown lads, perfectly capable of looking after themselves in what was essentially a wet field. All they had to do was cast around in a circle until they either saw the lights of Base Camp or crossed the track.

Their circle crossed nothing except marsh: all the same, all clinging and yielding and filled with sink-holes waiting for the unwary. Jimmy fell in one and Nick pulled him out, and they giggled uneasily. Nick fell in another and for a couple of minutes Jimmy couldn't get him out. They managed in the end, but the giggling stopped.

Nick tried to use his head. The wind had been blowing off the sea all day: if they walked with their backs to it, sooner or later they'd strike land. It might be an uncomfortable night but they'd be safe enough if they could just get out of this saltwater swamp. They'd work out where they were when the sun came up.

Then Nick lost his feet again and Jimmy, trying to save him, tumbled into the same pool. They found, as I had before them, that getting out was harder than getting in. When at last they had dragged one another over the edge they knew it had been a close thing – any harder and they might not have managed it. That was when real fear had set in. They hadn't dared go any further. They'd groped round for a firm spot, sat down back to back and waited to be rescued. And the prospect of rescue was only a little more attractive than the sink-hole.

After half an hour they saw lights. Five minutes later they were safe, marching back to Base Camp in disgrace.

The drama was over before we got back from Graveleigh, but the air of recrimination in the little hut was thick enough to cut with a knife. We exchanged significant glances, decided against further conversation and went to bed.

31

I woke up with a cold. Marion also had a bit of a cold, and Nick was streaming. It was hardly surprising, but it did nothing to lighten the atmosphere. It was like eating breakfast in a seal colony.

There was no talk until we finished the coffee. Then Chase said quietly, 'Without going over last night's events again I want to make two points. We call it a School of Adventure in deference to people like Nick's mum, but what we're running here are survival courses. We put you into dangerous situations and show you how to survive. Our supervision is vital to your safety. The marsh isn't a playground, it can kill – even people who know it, let alone folk who've come from safe, cosy little towns looking for a bit of fun.

'There's nothing wrong with a bit of fun. We *want* you to enjoy yourselves. But hauling dead bodies out of sink-holes is bad for our reputation. We can keep you safe but only if we know where you are and what you're doing. You're not children. We don't expect you to go sneaking off behind our backs.'

He looked round us, waiting for someone to argue. No one did.

'Which brings me to the second point. You're not prisoners here. You want to go into Graveleigh for a jar in the evening, you go. You don't need my permission. But I do need to know. OK, you left a note, which was better than nothing. But if you'd told me, I could have said, "Fine, but stick to the track, don't look for a shortcut"; and you'd have said, "Sure, no problem"; and I wouldn't have given you another thought. As it was, all the time we were looking for the water-babies I was wondering if, once we'd found them, we'd have to go out again looking for you.'

I had to concede he was right. 'We should have said. Next time we will.'

Hollis's chair grated as he got up. His voice grated too. 'Yesterday was the first day. We always make the first day easy. From now on you won't have the energy left for going down the pub in the evening.'

Maybe it was the instructors, determined to teach us a lesson; maybe it was the sobering effect of the previous night; maybe it was the rain, cold as charity, hard as nails. Whatever the reason, the moments of triumph and laughter that got us through the first day didn't survive into the second. A grimness settled on the party. It had never been a holiday; now it wasn't even a learning process so much as trial by ordeal.

The sheer physical exhaustion was mind-numbing. Muscles complained, then raged. But even with massive cramps we had to go on. Those who fell behind were encouraged, then harried, then bullied. Nothing – not entreaties, not threats, not tears – halted the remorseless progress of the day as we trudged through the wet wilderness, heads bent, lashed by the driving rain, chilled to the heart and weary to the bone.

The aim of the exercise, said Chase, was to show us how much more punishment we could absorb than we thought. Four hours out we understood the full implications of that. We'd signed over our basic human rights to these two men. I can't remember ever feeling so miserable. I don't cry easily but I cried then. No one noticed. We were all wet, muddy, and too damn tired to worry about anyone else.

No, that's not quite fair. George Fox, the fittest among us and the only one with energy to spare, circulated unobtrusively, helping where he could. But the bottom line was that each of us had somehow to scale the ramparts of his own exhaustion. George couldn't carry us over that barrier. Still, knowing he would have travelled faster alone, that he deliberately held the pace down for our benefit, helped.

A couple of times Costigian glanced round, weighing up the situation. But he said nothing.

By midday we were in serious trouble – from a medical standpoint, that is. I never doubted Chase's ability to bring us safe through the marsh. But the price we were paying was too high and still climbing.

I was most worried about Nick. His cold, which was hardly enough to take the shine off his face when we left Base Camp, was getting worse as he ran out of stamina. The expedition was finding all our weak spots. As time went on, we all went through what strength we had in reserve and then we were operating on the very substance of our bodies.

That's the wall that marathon runners talk of hitting. Until that point Nick's cold was a discomfort, nothing more. When he hit the wall, suddenly its significance burgeoned. Everyone looked exhausted, but Nick looked ill, dragging himself along in the rear because he wasn't strong enough to say he'd had enough.

And all the time Hollis was nagging him, revelling in the state he'd reduced him to. 'I thought you liked playing in the mud. It's fun, isn't it? Let's see you smile then. Only keep walking, because nobody's waiting for a big girl like you.' And I was too tired to do anything about it.

Not long after that we stopped. I thought maybe Chase had seen the state we were in and would have the sense to cut the thing short, but no. It was lunchtime. There'd be an hour's break while we ate.

We looked expectantly at him, then at Hollis, thinking that even another plate of beans would be welcome. But they appeared to have neither the provisions nor the means to cook them. Instead each produced from his pack a ball of twine, a penknife and a box of matches. Then they sat back and watched the understanding dawn.

'That's right,' said Chase. 'You want to eat, you catch something to eat.'

I know a little of what lives along the margins of the sea. 'Under no circumstances whatever,' I said flatly, weariness robbing the words of passion but not sincerity, 'do I intend to eat ragworm.'

Hollis shrugged. 'So catch something better.'

It was a mudflat, not the Dogger Bank. 'There's nothing better in there. The best angler in Britain couldn't catch anything I'd feed to our cat.' I drew myself up to my full if modest height, trying to judge where we were. 'Look, we can't be far from Graveleigh. We can probably buy something there.'

Hollis was doing the infuriating grin again. He patted the pockets of his jumpsuit. 'No money.'

'I'll get a loan from the publican.'

Chase said reasonably, 'You're not going to learn much about survival in the public bar of The Wake. Give the fishing a try. You'll be surprised what you can catch.'

All we were likely to catch was double pneumonia. But I wasn't going to fight this battle on my own. I'd wait until my companions discovered there are some lands you can't live off.

George helped himself to a couple of fathoms of line, set about disguising the hook as something a fish might fancy for its lunch, found a cleanish-looking stretch of drain and went fishing. Others, but not me, followed suit.

Nick sat in a miserable huddle of arms and knees and I went to see if I could do anything for him. I couldn't, but he appreciated the thought.

Then George let out a shrill whistle that turned all our heads, and he was struggling to land a catch that would have fed half Graveleigh. I ran to look but couldn't make out what it was through the murky water. At first I thought it was a game-fish, but actually it seemed to be more weight than fight that he was working to haul in.

When he landed it we could see why. It was a dead dog.

We looked at the dog. We looked at George. We looked at our instructors with hatred in our hearts. But Costigian was looking at the sky. 'Smoke.'

For a moment seven hearts quickened. Had someone set fire to Base Camp? But the direction, insofar as it was possible to gauge it out here with no points of reference, was wrong.

'Graveleigh?'

Costigian tilted his head. 'Over there.' So he at least had some idea where we were.

'What is it then?'

The tiniest smile lifted one corner of his mouth and his eyes were knowing. 'That chemical plant sounds a pretty big place. Big workforce. Sort of place that would need – for instance – a cafeteria. Showers. Possibly a bus.' And with that he turned away and began walking towards the plume of smoke.

He didn't get a dozen strides before I'd caught him up. I called back over my shoulder, 'I'll go with him – make sure he doesn't get lost.'

Another stride or two and Marion was with us, then Jimmy. Then, looking back, I saw George solemnly give Hollis the end of the string with the dead dog on it, link his arm through Nick's and come after us. Then we were all there, and as we climbed one slimy sodden bank that was identical to all the others the tip of a factory chimney hove into view.

II

Second Opinion

Five

This may not have been the first time Growth Industries had found mutinous survivalists on its doorstep. The security guard who let us through the gate looked more amused than alarmed at the sight of seven people in muddy jumpsuits with blacked-out faces. The idea that we might be industrial spies clearly never occurred to him. We asked for Dr Rodway and were directed to the main building.

You hear a lot about commercial architecture, none of it good. But compared with the virgin marsh around it, primordial and unspoilt, looking as it had for a thousand or a million years, the complex was a Garden of Eden. The red-brick walls were a splash of colour in the drab of the fen, and the windows that rose through three storeys had a crystal brightness that the drains and sink-holes couldn't match even when the sky was light enough to reflect in them.

More seductive still was the green. Lawns surrounded the buildings and rolled out to the boundary. There must have been acres of them, punctuated with island beds where roses grew in multicoloured profusion. Of course, if an agrochemicals firm couldn't fertilize to good effect, who could? We stumbled towards the building as if walking out of a desert.

Donald Rodway was trying hard not to laugh. He could have spared himself the effort: it wouldn't have added one iota to my humiliation. I was upholstered in mud and fluorescent nylon, my hair was in my face and my eyes were red with furious tears. I was so tired that if we'd been turned away I'd have sat down and sobbed. It was still raining steadily. Rodway held an umbrella over me and almost broke my heart.

I had been too weary to rehearse what I was going to say. Now words failed me. We weren't lost. We weren't in danger. Apart maybe from Nick, we weren't ill. We were just knackered. We'd had enough. But I didn't know how to say that to a man in polished shoes without sounding pathetic. I mumbled something like, 'Exhaustion . . . exposure . . . any chance of . . . ?' and hung my head in shame.

The doctor smiled kindly round our hopeful faces. 'Don't think you're the first. Still, seven at a time may be some kind of record.'

Perhaps a by-product of the industrial process, the hot water in the showers was endless. At first I stood under the torrent in my jumpsuit and the mud sluiced off me and down the drain. Then I did the same in my underwear. Finally I stripped down to just me and let the dancing stream massage the ache from my bones. The pleasure was exquisite. I felt my eyes closing and wondered if it was possible to fall asleep and drown in a shower.

There were no towels. I didn't much care, now I was warm I could drip-dry. But Marion reached in and altered the setting on my shower, and the hot water turned to jets of hot air blasting from the sides of the cubicle. There was also a clothes drier. When we met the men in the corridor we regarded one another in vast amusement, hardly recognizing these clean, cheerful people as our companions. Jimmy looked cleaner than when he got off the train. Nick's springy fair hair was standing almost vertically.

From there we headed to the canteen. It was like passing the wrong way through an abattoir, entering as dead meat and returning by degrees to a condition of blessed life. As we ate, we enthused about the facilities.

Rodway shrugged. 'We have to keep the workforce happy or they wouldn't stay. Not everyone wants to work in the middle of a bog: the least we can do is make sure they can get cleaned up afterwards.'

George looked surprised. 'People work in the marsh?'

'The maintenance department. The pipes running out to the terminal need attention sometimes. The electronics pick up problems as they develop, but solving them mostly means men in rubber trousers poking around in the mud.'

Which figured. All the clever technology that was meant to free men from the tyranny of difficult, dangerous, repetitive work, like all the other whizz-kids, quickly summed up which the best jobs were and took them. So the clever machines became managers and the difficult, dangerous, repetitive work was still largely done by men in rubber trousers. They were entitled to the best showers going.

'What pipes?' asked Costigian.

'They carry away the waste – industrial effluent. Did you notice the little brick lean-tos along the side of the building? That's where they go underground. We have a terminal on the shore and a ship calls every few weeks to take the waste away.'

'Like a bin lorry,' observed Marion.

Costigian was impressed. 'I guess it'd cost a fortune hauling it out by road, a truck at a time.'

'It was the main reason for building the plant here,' said Rodway. 'Sir Emlyn's idea – our chief executive, Sir Emlyn Wilson. He took over the family business thirty years ago and grew it into a major international player. It's still a family business, though. There are four sons and three grandchildren of his involved in running it. His eldest son Ernest is the company secretary.'

Thirty years ago the environmental lobby had been becoming an issue. By designing the plant around an efficient method of waste disposal GI had cleverly avoided a lot of the problems that had beset the chemical industry since.

Nick looked a lot better with a hot meal inside him, but before we left I took him quietly aside. 'While we're here, will you let Dr Rodway have a look at you? He might have something for that cold.'

The boy shook his head. 'I'm fine. It's only a cold.' A shadow almost like fear ghosted across his face then. 'What are they going to say when we go back?'

'If they've any sense at all,' I said shortly, 'very little. Now I've had a decent meal I'm ready for them. I'm a doctor too: I know what bodies can cope with, and I'm not going

41

to let them put us through that again. This isn't Devil's Island, we can leave any time we want to. If they want to run a postgraduate course for Green Berets, fine, but I'm out of here.'

The GI bus wasn't as noticeably odd as the Adventure School vehicle but it too made concessions to the conditions here, the chassis jacked up over big deep-cleated tyres. Of course, it would have to tackle the track across the marsh in winter when even survivalists had the sense to stay at home.

Rodway saw us off. I said, 'We haven't a farthing between us at the moment. But we'll be glad to pay for what we've used. Have someone let me know what we owe you. Apart from our lives, I mean.'

He smiled, demurring. 'You're very welcome. Like I said, GI's happy to contribute something to the life of the community. If there was more community, it'd contribute more. Since there's only Graveleigh and the survival school, we do what we can to help people stay in the village, and occasionally we help people get away from the school.'

We chuckled. Then, in case I got the idea he was criticizing them, he said, 'We're the best of friends really. Did you know GI has a stake in the Adventure School? Chase and Hollis used to work here. Before my time, of course.'

I was surprised neither of them had mentioned it. But we hadn't had much casual conversation. 'They're chemists?'

'Plant security. Before my time, but Chase was here for ten years after he left the Army. When he got the idea for the Adventure School the company helped him set it up. So if you get desperate enough to cut his throat with his own Swiss Army knife, it reflects badly on us. A bit of hot water and some lunch seems a small price to pay for avoiding that.'

Bumping over the causeway in the bus we discussed our next move. I'd have been glad to see the course fold. George, Marion and Costigian, for various reasons, wanted to complete but not at any price: they were prepared to leave if we couldn't agree a compromise. John Tarrant, and perhaps more surprisingly young Nick, said they wouldn't leave unless they were thrown out. John might eventually be beaten in the pursuit of his Army career but he wasn't going to surrender. And Nick had a school full of friendly rivals waiting to hear the gory details. He'd suffer anything for a week rather than admit that his prize got the better of him.

It was hard to know what Jimmy thought. He'd caught Nick's cold and everything he said came muffled through a handkerchief.

The consensus of opinion seemed to be that, if we could get Chase to make allowances for our varied but generally imperfect states of fitness, and the extra problems that the weather was giving us, we'd stick it out. Otherwise we'd call an all-terrain taxi.

George and I were deputed to do the talking: he because he could cope with anything the instructors could dream up, me because I could cope with next to nothing and wasn't shy about saying so. I was almost looking forward to it. I was ready for a showdown.

It didn't happen. As soon as we walked through the door of the Nissen hut I knew it wouldn't. Outside, the low driving cloud had soaked up the afternoon light so that it seemed almost evening. Inside, the stoves had been stoked to a rosy glow and Hollis was filling the kettle.

Chase glanced up as we came in. I looked for hostility, open and ready for a fight or battened down, waiting its opportunity. Instead I found only a little quiet humour in his eyes, neither hostile nor apologetic. 'Come and sit down; we need to talk.'

He said, 'What happened today wasn't very clever. I won't say it's the worst thing that's ever happened here, but losing one's platoon to a factory canteen is not the highlight of a military career.' The smile in his voice almost made it to his lips.

'I know we gave you a hard time. I meant to. Last night scared me: I wanted to make sure you all understood just how hostile an environment this is. I didn't want anyone thinking it's a playground. All the same, it was a misjudgement. I didn't realize how tired you were getting. Usually I can count on a chorus of complaints to warn me if a group's overstretched. I didn't allow for the fact that I wasn't the only one with a point to make about last night. This may

43

not be the fittest group we've ever had but it's got to be the most stubborn.'

And I swear, every one of us felt a little glow of pride.

'Anyway, letting the situation get out of hand was my mistake. It won't happen again. But for heaven's sake, if you can't do what I'm asking, say so. There's no prize for the first student to collapse of exhaustion. Mental toughness is valuable, but I don't want anyone making himself ill to prove how tough he is. You're not here to impress me. You're here to learn some skills, extend yourselves a bit, boost your self-confidence by seeing just how much you can cope with. Ending up in Accident & Emergency has no part in that.

'So I'm sorry if I pushed you so hard that strike action seemed the only answer. But if someone's having trouble keeping up, will they please *say* something? Don't go so stiff-upper-lipped on me that I don't know there's a problem until I see you marching away in a huff!'

I said, 'Um, yes, OK,' and George nodded; which proves how important it is for a group to have strong, articulate representation.

The point was, the man was right. If he'd made mistakes, so had we: we'd overreacted, at the wrong time and in the wrong way. None of us had come away with any glory. The only upside was that we were warmer, cleaner and better fed than we'd been for forty-eight hours. But tomorrow we were going to have to mend some fences.

I said, a shade tentatively, 'So what have you got in mind for tomorrow?'

Hollis brought the coffee. Chase smiled. 'Clio, you're really going to enjoy tomorrow.'

Breakfast was like an orientation lecture for the newly dead. The boys were honking and snorting like geese, Costigian had settled in a morose hump at one end of the table, Marion – bitter and edgy at the other – had eyeballs to match her hair and even George looked like a martyr, possibly Joan of Arc. John had caught the boys' cold.

I too felt like death warmed up. The cold had developed flu-like overtones, a hovering headache and a suggestion of joint cramps. I had slept badly, jarring fragments of chaotic dreams kept forcibly apart by racking, restless periods awake.

We pushed the eggs and beans round the plates with not much more enthusiasm than we'd shown for the dead dog. But the coffee went down rather better and by the time we'd drained the pot there was hope of resurrection.

I turned to Tom Chase. 'So what is it we're doing today that you wouldn't tell us about yesterday except for hinting that I'd like it?'

He grinned. He wasn't a man of notable good looks, and wouldn't have been twenty years ago: of modest height and build, more wiry than muscular, with a narrow rather forgettable face. But there was something about him that impressed. In a world full of big twisters and little ones, he struck me as a straight man. His mistakes were honest ones. The grin, and the intelligent eyes, were attractive in his unremarkable face.

He said, 'You're going out with a hooker called Granny.'

She was a Galway hooker and she was called *Grainne*. The name, in fancy Celtic script, was painted white on her tar-black bow. She had a fat black hull and a suit of heavy dark sails, and she had to be a hundred years old. I fell in love while Chase was still parking the bus.

She'd been built on the west coast of Ireland to catch fish and carry supplies out to the Aran Isles, and it was impossible to guess the succession of events that had brought her from that wild western ocean to Hunstanton. Now she belonged to a pop singer and the Adventure School chartered her for a day each week to teach city-dwellers the art of handling a sea-going vessel solely on the strength of men's muscles.

Of the two of them, Terry Hollis was the sailor. Chase was an adequate crewman but he lacked the skill to skipper *Grainne*. Hollis had the skills, but I thought he'd gained them in offshore racers, all GRP and carbon fibre, because he handled the hooker as if all the years in her timbers and all the miles under her keel were a handicap rather than a joy.

The solid rain had given way to blustery showers, big

dark-edged clouds sailing across a pale sky and the odd blink of watery sun between. Quite soon we were as wet as we'd ever been and probably colder. But it's different on a boat. Cleaner.

We hadn't been aboard twenty minutes when young Jimmy turned a delicate shade of primrose, announced faintly that he felt sick and stumbled to the nearest gunwale. It was too late to warn him. We waited till he'd finished, then steered him to the stern rail: vomiting upwind is never a good idea. We left him clinging to the rail.

The wind bellied out the dark sails and the little ship dug her shoulder into the sea, and when the squalls came she hunched down and plugged on like a dowager duchess playing American football. I thought then that I didn't care what the rest of the week had in store. These fleeting spells when the rain eased and the sun shone and the old hooker with her rigging a-thrum ploughed a white furrow across the pewter Wash were fair payment for all the miserable hours that had gone before and probably lay ahead. So I believed.

Chase called the length of the well, 'How about it? Can we get down to Graveleigh?'

Hollis glanced at the masthead pennant and nodded. 'Yeah, I can do that.'

Because of the ocean-going tankers visiting GI, I knew there was deep water close inshore. The north-east wind was the problem. I said, 'It'll be a weary old beat back out.'

Hollis grinned at me, not pleasantly. 'You're not worried about a rough ride, are you, Clio?'

'This isn't a twelve-metre, Terry, she won't point upwind. You take us on to a lee shore, we'll spend the rest of the week working her back. Actually, that suits me fine. But think how many chances you'll miss to throw us in the mud.'

Chase had come back to join us, looking from me to Hollis and back, trying to judge who was right. 'What do you think, Terry? Would we be better heading across the Wash instead? We don't want to get trapped.'

It didn't matter a scrap to Terry Hollis, but he wasn't taking orders from a student. He growled, 'There's no problem. It'll take longer coming up than going down, that's all.'

Chase explained. 'It makes a nice day if we can get down to Graveleigh and see the marsh from the sea. All at once it makes a kind of sense if you can see how the saltings developed.'

I nodded. 'I'm not complaining. But this old lady isn't going to beat ten miles up wind in a couple of hours.'

The thing about sailing boats is all the variables. Maybe they'd never had the wind those few points north of east that made Graveleigh a dead run before. Or maybe when they'd had that they'd also had the tide pushing them out when they wanted to leave. Or maybe I was wrong, but I didn't think so. I've sailed traditional boats before, and while they'll take anything the sea can throw at them, they also take their time and waste a handful of degrees every time they go about. Those big full-cut sails need to be kept round and full of wind. Any modern yacht will point higher than *Grainne* could hope to. Fighting the tide as well, the old hooker would just keep sailing across the wind, making no distance over the seabed between one tack and the next.

But Chase didn't know that, and if Hollis knew he wanted to prove me wrong.

'Tell you what,' said Chase, 'we'll go down to Graveleigh but we'll leave early, allow ourselves time to get home. OK?' Hollis nodded negligently. I wasn't bothered either: I'd rather spend the night on *Grainne* than at Base Camp.

The marsh appeared as a low smudge ahead of us, thickening and darkening until what Saul Penny called The Island began to lift out of it. It wasn't so much the height you noticed – not even a Dutchman would have called it a hill – as the broken skyline, the angles created by the little roofs. As we drew closer, the line of the harbour wall was visible.

From here we could see the GI terminal. The jetty must have been half a mile long, a steel tracery woven by an architectural spider, a glittering silver span racing out over the grey shallows where The Wash was thinking of becoming salt marsh. At the seaward end there was a building with great tanks that went down to the seabed, the draught of a sea-going ship below. The terminal was the key to the whole operation. The waste filling those great vats could be shifted no other way.

We cruised along the hem of the marsh for a while, far enough out to stay off the mud but close enough to pick out the shattered remnants of the Squire's house and the rounded roof of Base Camp. Then we tightened up and began to head out to sea again. *Grainne* lay down into the wind and by degrees we left the shore behind. Hollis leered at me as if expecting an apology. But it was slack water. Soon now the tide would start to flood. They say that when the tide comes in over the silts of The Wash it travels faster than a man can run.

George came on deck with a proper rod that he'd found below and tried his hand at fishing again. Chase started the stove. I admired his optimism, but George landed his first mackerel before the pan was hot and reeled in the next half-dozen as quickly as he could get the line baited. We set up a production line: George caught them, Costigian despatched them, Marion gutted them and John cooked them. We washed them down with cans of shandy that, lacking a fridge, we trailed on string behind the boat.

About then I realized that the flood was running. *Grainne*'s use of the wind and water had altered not at all, but now the sea itself was heading for the marsh the mathematics had changed. I watched the shore over a couple of long tacks and reckoned we were covering the same ground each time. We'd sailed into a pocket and we were going to stay here, sailing up and down, until the tide slackened five hours from now.

I looked at Hollis and said nothing. I didn't have to: the thought went all the way.

Distinctive sounds reached me from the lee rail and I supposed that the increased buffeting of the beat had got to Jimmy again. But it was Nick. His face was white and slick with a cold sweat, his eyes startled. 'I must have got a bad fish.'

It was possible but it would have been a fast reaction. I suspected it was more to do with how he'd been feeling this morning and the cold – if it was a cold – he'd started the day before. I took Chase aside. 'What do you think? Is it just the different diet, different activities, or is he ill?'

Chase shrugged uneasily. 'We do get acclimatization symptoms with the students – a bit of sickness, gyppy tummy, chills. Never anything serious. Survival training is stressful, it's very different from what most people are used to; it can give them an uncomfortable day or two while they adjust. About Nick, I'm not sure. He looks worse than that to me.'

I thought so too. It could have been flu he'd been incubating; it's a nastier disease than those who haven't had it tend to think and could have accounted for his symptoms. But something in the presentation wasn't really flu either. I wished I'd had Rodway examine him.

There were bunks down below and I thought about settling him in one for the long beat home. But close confines and stale air are the worst thing for anyone who's feeling sick. So I wrapped him warmly in a blanket and wedged him in a corner of the cockpit.

There were two spots of colour in the pallor of his cheeks and his skin felt cold and clammy. His breath was coming fast and not going very deep, and his eyes were slow to focus. Except for the lack of an obvious cause it looked like shock. He remained queasy but there was no marked tenderness around his abdomen. He didn't react to my fingers probing for the appendicitis reflex except with a look of indignation.

I gave him my most reassuring smile. 'Maybe it was the fish. Sue the cook.'

Chase was waiting anxiously for a report. 'Do you know what it is?'

'No. To be honest, I don't.'

'Serious?'

'I don't know. He's feeling rotten but that's not necessarily the best guide. If it was something he ate, he might start coming round now he's got rid of it. Maybe it was just a cold until he got a touch of food poisoning on top. I don't know. But I don't want to be still out here six hours from now.' If I was wrong about the appendicitis, the boy would need to be on an operating table long before *Grainne* would stagger back into Hunstanton.

Chase said quietly, 'How long do we have?'

I wasn't being much help but I was reluctant to commit myself when I knew little more than he did. 'It depends what the problem is. If he doesn't get any worse, he'll be all right however long it takes us to get home. If he starts feeling better, he could be back to normal by tonight. But if he deteriorates, I'll need to get him ashore within the next hour.'

'And we can't be back on the mooring inside an hour, can we?' Chase made the only possible decision. 'All right. We'll stop trying to fight our way home and run back into Graveleigh. That'll be the quickest way to get him ashore, won't it?'

I nodded. With the wind and tide behind us we'd be there in half an hour. 'We can get help at The Wake. Leave Nick and me ashore and you can sail *Grainne* back in her own time. If you wait until the tide turns, she'll make the passage easily enough.'

So the old hooker turned her black haunches on the open sea and spread her dark sails wide. For three hours she'd been battling against wind and tide and made perhaps a couple of miles north-east. Now she was heading south-west again they were back on the same side: the force was gone out of the wind, the violence out of the sea, and she creamed on down towards The Island as obligingly as a horse heading for home.

The tiled roofs of Graveleigh grew above the dark line of the harbour wall. There was a channel of a kind, but it wasn't marked: the only people using it were locals who knew where it was. But Hollis was an accurate pilot. Steering a big boat through a narrow channel with wind and sea behind you takes a good eye and a steady nerve, and those were virtues he had. We dropped the sails and came in on the engine, and tied her up against the fishing boat.

For quarter of an hour I'd been too busy to do more than check that my patient was still where I'd left him in the well. Now, as I looked round, Costigian climbed to his feet with Nick in his arms. The boy was barely conscious. Costigian said quietly, 'We need to hurry.'

Chase had a mobile phone in his dry kit. 'I'll call the plant, have Dr Rodway meet us.' But he couldn't get a signal. He gave up after a couple of minutes' trying. 'This happens sometimes. I'm not sure if it's the coverage, the terrain, or what. They used to say at the plant that the phones go down when they scrub out the number 5 condenser. Let's take him to The Wake – it'll be quicker.'

Six

I don't know if the pub was open when we arrived. The door wasn't locked but there was no one in the bar – neither Saul Penny nor the old man who meant to die on his corner stool. Chase went looking for a phone, I went to look for Saul.

I tried the door behind the bar. 'Saul, are you there?'

But he wasn't. The room was a little chintzy bedroom backing on to the harbour. I could see *Grainne*'s mast through the net curtain and a collection of old-fashioned ornaments ranged along the window sill. A woman's voice said, 'Who is it? Come in.'

I said, 'It's Clio Marsh. I'm looking for Saul. I've got a sick boy outside.'

If I hadn't known that the woman in the bed was Saul's mother I'd have taken her for his grandmother. Probably she wasn't much older than me. But she looked like an old lady: faded eyes, skin the colour of talcum powder, a frailty of narrow shoulders under a shawl. Her hair was white on the pillow where she'd been resting when I woke her. Her voice was reedy-thin, the local accent gone to a flute in it. But her eyes were intelligent, only very tired. Ill health might have sapped her body but she had beaten off its attacks on her mind.

I found myself thinking, That poor boy! He's a cripple himself, he's looking after an invalid mother and this place which is his business, and his home is slowly dying under him. No wonder he's bitter.

'Saul's down in the cellar,' said Mrs Penny. 'What's the matter? That's *Grainne* in the harbour. Were you on her?'

I hadn't time to fill in a questionnaire but it seemed rude

to leave without an explanation. 'We're from the Adventure School. We were out sailing when one of the group was taken ill. I need to phone for an ambulance. Is that all right?'

'Of course it is,' she nodded, 'help yourself. And see, there's some blankets in that box – take him one. The least we can do is keep him warm.'

Saul must have heard our voices because as I left his mother's room the other door behind the bar opened and his shaggy head appeared from the cellar. 'What's going on?' So I told him too, and by then Chase had returned from the phone.

'The doctor's on his way.'

Out of the wind and the constant movement, Nick was looking a little better – enough to be embarrassed by the fuss. He kept muttering, 'It was just a bad fish. I'll be all right tomorrow.'

Chase was watching him uneasily. I said, 'What's worrying you?'

'I'm wondering what to do about the boat.'

'I told you: wait for the tide to turn and take her home.'

But he'd thought it out more carefully than I had. 'And what if an hour or so out someone else goes down with this? What if it's nothing to do with the fish, if it's this bug you've all had? Nick was the first to start with it. What if everyone who's had a runny nose is going to collapse? What if we're five miles from land when they start dropping like flies?'

I'd been stupid not to see it. It wasn't a risk he could take. I nodded wearily. 'Sorry – I'm a bit below par myself. You're right. We don't know that this thing is catching but we can't assume it isn't. We should act as if we're all potential victims, at least for another twenty-four hours. You'd better leave *Grainne* where she is till we see what's going to happen.'

'Yes,' he decided. 'I'll get back to the boat, tell everyone what we're doing. The doctor will be here in a couple of minutes – don't wait for us, I'll find some transport and we'll follow you to the plant. I'd like Dr Rodway to check everyone over once he's finished with Nick.'

Because I wasn't firing on all cylinders I hadn't worked out what he meant until he had gone. 'He called Rodway, then, not an ambulance?'

Costigian shrugged. 'He'll be here sooner. We can take him on to a hospital if the doc wants him there.'

'I'm not going to hospital,' mumbled Nick plaintively. 'I got a bad fish, that's all. I'll be all right tomorrow.'

I asked Costigian how he was feeling.

'All right. I had a headache this morning but the sea air seems to have cleared it. Why?'

'I'm still trying to work out what the problem is. Everyone looked like death warmed up this morning. Coincidence, or because we've all had a touch of what Nick's got?'

'The flu?'

'If that's what it is.'

'What else?'

I resented being interrogated. I didn't know what was wrong – with Nick or any of us. I wasn't a doctor any more, hadn't practised for a decade. My medicine chest at home was identical to everyone else's, crammed with half-used bottles of aspirin, that adhesive tape that sticks to every surface except skin, and tacky bottles of honey-and-lemon mixture as used by your grandmother and never bettered. Medicine was no longer my field.

But faced with suffering, you can't opt out. Maybe solicitors can stop practising law by closing the front door; maybe estate agents never find themselves conducting an emergency valuation. But a doctor's bag is like Pandora's Box: once you've opened it, everything changes for ever. You have obligations you can never completely evade. If someone is hurt or sick and there isn't a real doctor on hand – a proper doctor, a doctor who knows his humerus from his gluteus maximus without reference to *Gray's Anatomy* – it's your problem. You deal with it as best you can.

I felt responsible. I should have found the answer before this – before Nick was this ill and a question mark hung over the rest of us. I'd been there from the start, seen the first symptoms and watched them develop, and I'd still no more idea whether the problem was bacterial, viral, toxic or black magic than I'd had yesterday morning when Nick started blowing his nose. I felt I'd let everyone down.

When I got round to answering Costigian's question, the

answer was short on facts and short in manner. 'I don't know what's wrong with him. I don't know what's wrong with me, or what caused your headache, or if it's all the same thing or if we're just getting assorted symptoms because we're under stress. All right? I don't know.'

Saul Penny said, 'It's marsh fever.'

I glared round at him. 'What?' I might not have practised for ten years but I still knew more medicine than a village publican.

Except that Saul had spent his life here. If there was something in the fen capable of causing an illness – a biting insect, perhaps, conceivably a marsh gas – Saul would know about it. He might not have a scientific name for it, but he'd recognize it when he saw it. 'You've seen this before?'

'Headache, cold, no energy, then you start a temperature? That's marsh fever all right.' His light tenor voice was confident. 'You may have a fancier name for it but that's what it is.'

'Do you see much of it?'

'We don't see much of anything round here. Island folk don't get it. Bird-watchers get it, mostly.'

'Bird-watchers?'

'They're the only ones daft enough to spend much time in that bog. They come looking for marsh harriers and somebody's godwit. If they come for longer than a day, they stay here – there's nowhere else. If they stay two days, the second day they start a cold and ask me for hot whisky. If they stay three days, they go to the shop for paracetamol. I can't remember when anybody stayed four days.'

That fitted with how the rest of us were feeling, even if it didn't explain why Nick was so much worse. I said to Costigian, 'If something in the marsh causes it, why hasn't Chase seen it before? Come to that, why hasn't Chase got it?'

Saul had the answer to that too. 'Don't see it much in summer.'

And the Adventure School didn't operate in winter. But the bird-watchers did?

'They come looking for winter visitors. All sorts winter

on the mudflats. And then if we get a windy week, things you wouldn't normally see here blow in from the continent. So there's always a few twitchers on the look-out for occasionals.'

It was a whole subculture I knew nothing of. I only know three birds and one of them's an ostrich. 'But if it's only winter twitchers who get marsh fever, why have we got it?'

Saul shrugged and lurched away on his crutches. 'How would I know? I thought you were the doctor.'

People did keep making that mistake.

Costigian gave a helpless shrug. 'Maybe we're reading too much into it. Nick's the only one who's really ill: maybe it *was* the fish. If everybody's feeling better tomorrow, it was just one of those things and we'll never know what caused it.'

And I hoped he was right but was afraid he was wrong.

The car drawing up outside was Rodway's 4x4. I tucked the blanket around my patient. 'Soon have you in bed.'

He managed a feeble grin. Costigian went to help him up, but Nick got to his feet unaided and walked to the door.

Donald Rodway was coming into The Wake as we were going out. I saw his gaze, professionally astute, take in Nick's colour, the beading of sweat on his skin and the slight weary wobble as he walked to the car. 'Let's get this young man to my office and sort out what's troubling him.'

'Tom Chase wants you to give everyone a once-over, see if anyone else is likely to go down with it.'

'That's a sensible precaution,' agreed Rodway. 'You two come with us, why don't you? I'll send the minibus for the others.'

When the red bricks and green lawns of Growth Industries came at us out of the monotone fen, I felt as Arabs must on seeing the towers of a desert city rise out of the sand.

Costigian and I settled ourselves in the canteen and waited to be called. I hadn't had a medical examination for years and I wasn't keen on having one now. And I had nothing to hide. 'What are you going to tell Rodway about the hole in your shoulder?' I asked.

He frowned, one heavy brow ducking low over the thoughtful, intelligent eye. 'What do you mean?'

'He's bound to notice and he's going to ask. I don't think you can keep it a secret any longer.'

His expression didn't alter. 'Just because you don't know doesn't make it a secret.'

But I'd seen the pain he'd swallowed rather than talk about it. 'If I can't find out, *that* makes it a secret.'

He chuckled at that, the laughter a deep rumble in his throat, and relented. 'Clio, if it's the only way you're going to sleep nights, I'll tell you. An eighteen-year-old kid did it, and he did it with my gun. It's kids and women get you every time. If he'd been a six-footer with a broken nose and fists like the shovels on a D7 I wouldn't have taken my eye off him. But because he was a kid, and he was scared, and I didn't think he was going any place, I dropped my guard.'

I pursed my lips. 'You lied to me. I asked you if you were a policeman, and you lied. Didn't you?'

'Not exactly,' he said. 'I was a policeman. I mean to be one again. Right now I'm not. Not in any meaningful sense.'

It had been a serious injury: of course he hadn't been back on the beat the next week. 'These things take time.'

'Yeah? Well, I haven't *got* much time.'

'*Make* time. Costigian, you could have been killed.'

For some reason that made him laugh, although I don't think he found it funny. 'Yes, I could. It *should* have been me that died – it was my mistake. Instead of which I'm stuck with a crappy shoulder and a medical board who want me to take a desk job.'

So that was it. That was why it was worth putting himself through hell. He'd made a mistake and someone had died, and now he was desperate to prove – to himself and anyone else who doubted it – that he could still do his job. That was why he had to get the shoulder working again, and why there was a deadline.

'You've got a medical coming up?'

He nodded. 'I'm going home next month. If I can pass fit, I can have my old job back.'

'And if you can't?'

57

'I'm sure as hell not spending the next twenty years in an office. The shoulder's not a problem. I could lose the arm and still be a good cop.'

I didn't doubt it. I hadn't known him long, but I knew he was a good cop. The Royal Canadian Mounted Police knew it too and wanted to keep him on staff. But he didn't want the only kind of work they could offer an injured man. He saw the desk job as putting him out to pasture, but the streets aren't the only place where important policing is done.

But you can't tell a man what's good for him. It's the second thing a girl learns about the opposite sex. He'll blame you for being wrong and never forgive you for being right. But I'd be sorry if Costigian threw a job he could do well on to the funeral pyre of one he couldn't do any more.

Donald Rodway came back. I could see from his tiny puzzled frown that he hadn't solved the mystery of the boking survivalist at a glance, the way they do in hospital stories starring doctors called Craig. I asked, 'How is he?'

'Feeling better, I think. His temperature's up but he seems stable enough. Maybe it is flu. I've put him to bed – I'll keep him here for twenty-four hours or so. I think he's over the worst but I'll keep an eye on him until we're sure.' He smiled, an amused glance going between us. 'So who's first for the inspection pit?'

Costigian made a gesture of gentlemanly deference, but I was having none of it. 'I'll stay here till Nick's on the mend. If that's all right with you, Doctor?'

'Certainly, Doctor,' agreed Rodway solemnly.

'So you can give my friend his MOT while I finish the coffee. Don't worry about the extra holes in him – they're honourable scars.'

Seven

It took Rodway an hour to check everyone out. Afterwards we talked for another hour, but we were no wiser at the end than at the beginning. It was clear that the group was affected by a pathogen causing a disease similar to, though not exactly like, influenza. Nick had it worst. John was noticeably unwell, so that Rodway asked him too to stay overnight at the clinic. The rest of us had nothing more to report than runny noses, the odd headache, and muscular aches and pains that might have had more to do with the exertions of the last few days.

The fact that neither Chase nor Hollis had symptoms was interesting. Everywhere the seven of us had been since we came together, they'd been too. They'd been as cold as us, as wet as us, had eaten the same food and slept in the same building. Any bug we'd met they must have met as well. The obvious inference was that Saul Penny was right: it was something in the marsh that affected visitors who hadn't had time to get used to it.

So the twitchers got it when they came in pursuit of winter visitors, and survivalists who came in the milder days of summer got a touch of it. Only Chase thought it was just holiday tummy. Saul called it marsh fever, and until we could identify it that was probably as good a name as any. A biting insect was the most likely vector. It was puzzling that it bit more in winter, when insects are mostly dormant, than in summer, when they swarm everywhere. But an entomologist could probably identify the reason and the insect both.

Rodway thought both Nick and John would be feeling better by morning and doubted if anyone else would be any worse. He expected we'd be fit to sail *Grainne* home on the morning tide.

The bus took all who were going back to Base Camp, then returned to collect the day shift and take them to the greater comfort of their homes beyond the marsh. There weren't as many of them as the size of the complex suggested. Much of the work was automated. Machines don't get tired and careless, or complain about the smell, or catch marsh fever. But as Rodway had said, they're not very good at thumping pipes with a monkey wrench either.

Thinking about that, I left the canteen and padded along to the clinic – padding because I had wedged my trainers behind a radiator in the hope of drying them out. The clinic ran to three two-bedded rooms and an office/surgery where I found Rodway bent over his paperwork. The door was open so I tapped and walked in. He looked up. 'Bored already?'

'Of course not. Watching chemicals turn into fertilizer has to be the most exciting night out since they stopped snail-racing at the White City. I had trouble dragging myself away long enough to give this thing some thought.'

'Did you find any answers?'

'No,' I admitted, 'but I came up with a good question. The men you installed the showers for – the guys who tap pipes and get muddy – do they catch marsh fever?'

Rodway frowned. 'Not in the time I've been here, but that's only a couple of months. Maybe they get it in winter. Or maybe they're resistant, like Chase and Hollis. If they meet this thing often enough, they may build up an immunity.'

'Maybe their rubber trousers stop the insects biting.' Our fluorescent jumpsuits, while possibly more dashing, weren't waterproof, so anything that was in the water had access to us.

'Could be,' nodded Rodway. 'They're certainly well protected – they have to be if they're dealing with leaks: the toxins in those pipes are pretty lethal. The suit comes with a built-in respirator. They say you could walk on the moon in it.'

60

'Apart from the men checking the pipes, does anyone else here spend time in the marsh?'

The doctor shook his head. 'The staff come in by road – nobody lives close enough to walk. All the processing is done in the plant: the finished product leaves on lorries, the waste leaves by pipe. There's a security team who occasionally drive round the perimeter or down to the terminal, but nobody else works outside.'

So the only GI people who worked in the marsh were proof against anything it might throw at them. The people in Graveleigh either worked the remaining fishing boats or stayed in the village: they might have developed an immunity or they might never meet the pathogen. I still had no idea what it was. 'Should we send a blood sample for testing?'

Rodway opened the door of his fridge. Phials were labelled with Nick's and John's names and the date. Maybe a path lab would track down whatever was responsible for their illness. I couldn't think what else we could do.

Rodway had a flat in Spalding, but he didn't leave people in the clinic overnight without supervision. He had the two boys in one room, meant to sleep in another and showed me to the third. When I'd said I was staying I hadn't realized he intended to. I felt a bit surplus to requirements now.

But the bus had gone and I wasn't walking back to Base Camp, so I settled down on the bed with a copy of the *Lancet* that brought home to me just how long I'd been out of the body business. I felt like a coachman desperately trying to mug up on the internal combustion engine because the mistress had swapped her horses for an automobile. I felt sure they'd changed the layout of the alimentary system since I was last inside one.

About seven o'clock, tiring of medical jargon, I pottered next door to the boys' room. Nick was asleep, curled under a duvet with only the top of his head showing, but John was awake and leafing through a copy of *Time*. He looked better but not a lot more cheerful.

Then I saw what was behind his wan expression. There was a feature in the magazine on the Green Berets training in the Central American jungle. 'Do you ever get the feeling,' he said, his voice low to avoid disturbing Nick, 'that life is dropping you some pretty hefty hints?'

The dream was over. He'd done his best. He'd tried to be a soldier but he wasn't strong enough. Not only had he failed to come through the induction, he'd failed to survive the survival course meant to toughen him up for it.

I tried to tell him it was just bad luck, that even Green Berets get ill if the wrong bug bites them, but he wasn't looking for sympathy. He'd reached his decision. 'I swore I wouldn't quit till I was thrown out, but the time comes when it's just plain silly to keep banging your head on the same brick wall.'

He smiled as if he was almost relieved to have the thing settled even if it hadn't worked out as he wanted. 'Let's face it, there are seven of us on this course: a schoolboy, a layabout, two women, a man with a bad shoulder, a lorry-driver and me. Apart from George I'm the fittest one here – I've trained the hardest, I'm closest to my peak. But when we all get the same bug, only the schoolboy gets sicker than me. If that's not a hint I don't know what is.'

I might have argued with him but in fact I thought he was right. 'I'm sorry.'

He shrugged. 'It's been coming. Now I have to deal with it. I've wasted enough time – now I'm going to find something I can do well.'

I didn't doubt it. 'Will you finish the week here?'

He shook his head. 'There's no point. I'll get a lift back to civilization tomorrow, start working on something with a future.' He grinned, vividly. 'My mum and dad'll be so proud when I tell them I've finally dropped out of something!'

I was returning to my room when I sensed rather than heard someone behind me and, turning quickly, found myself almost in the arms of a narrow man in a grey suit whom I hadn't seen before.

That wasn't altogether surprising. Apart from Dr Rodway, the canteen ladies and the man on the gate I'd met no one here. There was something surreal about how few people worked in the place. Of course, the clinic would naturally be located at the quiet end of the plant.

Before I had time to wonder who he was, the man introduced himself. 'I'm sorry if I startled you, Dr Marsh. I'm Ernest Wilson.'

'The company secretary,' I remembered.

He gave a minimal smile. 'You've had the introductory lecture, I see.'

I nodded. 'It's an impressive place you have here. And still a family firm.'

'Yes indeed. Everything we have today we owe to my father. And he's still in his office most days until six.'

'The marsh fever hasn't done him much harm, then.'

He wasn't sure if it was a joke. He just said, 'No. I wondered how our guests were, and if there was anything you needed.'

People who don't get jokes will never get them however carefully you explain. It's always a mistake to try. And something about Ernest Wilson discouraged that kind of intimacy. The narrowness, and the greyness, were constantly repeating themes. He had a narrow grey face cut in planes like a modern sculpture, and sharp grey eyes, and hair just turning grey clipped ruthlessly short. His large-framed spectacles might have been black but in fact they were dark grey. Under the grey suit was an impeccably white shirt and a grey tie.

'I think they'll live,' I said. 'The boy's asleep, which is the best way of dealing with most illness. Tarrant's looking better, he should be fine tomorrow. Dr Rodway may want to keep Nick another day, but we'll be out of your hair after that.'

He raised an eyebrow as fine as if it had been plucked. The precision of his speech suggested he had once been told that careless talk costs lives, or even money. 'Please don't think we want to be rid of you. We're glad our facilities have been of use. We need to maintain a clinic here but it doesn't see many patients. Rodway will have been glad to do some real doctoring for once.'

We parted then. Wilson went down the corridor and tapped at the surgery door, and I returned to my room. I didn't hear him leave, but then I hadn't heard him arrive. About ten o'clock I turned the light out, and I slept like a log until someone came hammering at my door in the small hours.

John was struggling into his clothes even as he waited for me to open the door. His face was white and urgent in the glare of the corridor lights.

'Wha-a-a-? Who . . . ?' I tried again. 'What time is it?'

Like a soldier, he wore his wristwatch twenty-four hours a day. 'Two thirty. Clio, have you seen Nick?'

I stared at him. 'Of course not. Isn't he . . . ?' But if he'd been in his bed John wouldn't have woken me. I was barely decent. I left the door ajar, talking through it, while I searched for my clothes. 'When did you see him last?'

'Maybe an hour ago. He woke me up. I think he was sleep-walking. He was sort of vague and seemed to be looking for something. I told him to go back to bed, we'd find it in the morning, and he did. But then a few minutes ago I woke up again and his bed was empty. I wondered if maybe he'd felt worse and come looking for you.'

By now I was dressed. John was clearly anxious and I was too: a sick boy sleepwalking in a chemical plant was a situation that needed addressing. 'He's not been here. Come on, we'll try Rodway's room.'

But the doctor too was sleeping until we woke him, and had seen and heard no one. We combed the immediate area without success. 'We'd better get some help,' said Rodway.

At once everyone who wasn't needed to ensure the safety of the plant was taken off production and organized into a search that swept from the clinic through the office block and towards the laboratories and factory. After an hour we were fairly sure he was no longer in the building. Every door that wasn't locked had been opened and there was no sign of him.

'But why would he go outside?' asked John.

'If he was feverish,' I said, 'he might not have needed much of a reason. Looking for something he thought he'd lost. Or maybe he thought he should be back at Base Camp – that they'd be looking for him, that he'd be in trouble again.'

Rodway's eyes met mine. He was thinking the same thing. 'My God.'

'Could he have got past the gate?'

'I don't know. It's mostly for show – nobody comes here except the workforce. There's a gateman, but it's not Fort Knox. I've come in without being seen.'

A chill settled through my spine. 'So we've got a delirious boy trying to make his way across the marsh alone in the dark. Donald, we have to find him.'

We were in the processing plant by now, the rumble of machinery a constant backdrop. He picked up the nearest phone. 'The security guys have all-terrain vehicles; they'll cover the ground faster than we can on foot. And I'll call the Adventure School so they can start looking for him at their end.'

He managed a tight smile. 'Don't worry, Clio, we'll find him. He may not have got as far as the marsh. When we search the compound we'll maybe find him curled up under a rose bush.' But we didn't.

A throaty growl heralded the arrival of the ATVs. They were essentially motorbikes, steered by handlebars, with two seats fore-and-aft and four big doughnut wheels with enough tread to get traction on any surface. There were four of them. Twin headlights stabbed out powerfully from each.

There was nothing more I could do at Growth Industries. Rodway was going to stay at the plant so when Nick was found there would be no delay in treating him. I thought the best thing I could do was get to Base Camp in case he arrived there. Rodway had someone drive me there in a Land Rover and John came too.

Unlike the ATVs the Land Rover had to stay on the road. At least, it was a rough road heading west from GI; the branch that peeled off towards Base Camp was no more than a track. The wind was half a gale now, hurling the rain at the windscreen like bullets, too hard and fast for the wipers to clear it.

We were still some way from Base Camp when we saw the flicker of torches picking across the marsh like a squadron of glow-worms. They were moving line abreast, ten or fifteen yards apart, the torches weaving from side to side. John tapped the driver's shoulder. 'Let me off here. I'll join on the end of the line.' He took the torch from the Land Rover's kit.

We waited in the driving rain for the line to reach us. I wanted to tell Chase I'd be at Base Camp if they found him, and the driver had been told to stay with me in case I needed transport in a hurry. The glow-worms inched towards us.

John was flashing his torch around as we waited. Then the scanning beam stopped abruptly and I heard his breath catch. 'Clio . . .'

He'd got this far. Another half-mile – less, even – and he'd have followed the track up the front steps of Base Camp. But his strength, sapped by illness, had given out and he'd stumbled into the drain. Or else in his fevered mind he'd seen lights or heard voices, and thought to take a short cut across the bog. For whatever reason, this close to safety he had turned off the muddy track and chanced himself to the fen.

And now he floated face down in the drain, a still thing dark in the dark water that could have been a log if we hadn't been searching for a missing boy. And he was dead. He had to be dead: if this had just happened our headlights would have picked him up as he stumbled off the road. He couldn't have been there less than two or three minutes, might have been there for an hour.

But you can't afford to make assumptions. People falling into cold water lose body heat and their need for oxygen falls too. People have been revived after remarkable lengths of time because the water was cold enough. I started toward the drain. My teeth were chattering: I was trying to explain all this, to explain the urgency, but the words were coming out all fractured.

It hardly mattered. John dropped the torch and went into the drain feet first without waiting for instructions. It must have been four feet deep. But he fastened one hand in Nick's hair and hauled his face out of the water, and by then I was on my knees on the edge, reaching to help him. The driver hurried round the front of the Land Rover and together we dragged the limp thing that had been Nick Baker, unexpectedly heavy now it was waterlogged, up on to the road.

He had to be dead. I didn't believe he could be that limp and that heavy and that still, and some flicker of life remain in him. But for more than ten minutes I acted as if he was alive. I breathed air into him and pumped water out. I worked his chest to coax a little activity out of his heart. There was no pulse that I could feel, but he was cold and I was cold and the nearest ECG was twenty miles away. I couldn't take the chance of being wrong. I went on thumping him and massaging him and breathing for him until, the cold notwithstanding, sweat mingled with the rain that dripped from my face on to his bare chest.

Then hands on my shoulders stilled my efforts and drew me to my feet, and the soft burr of a transatlantic accent was saying, 'He's gone, Clio.' I let Costigan lead me away like a child, and until he silently passed me his handkerchief I was not aware that some of the sweat running down my face was tears.

Eight

We took him back to Growth Industries. It seemed a more appropriate last resting place than the glorified tin hut that was Base Camp. All we could do for him now was afford him a little dignity in which to wait for the ambulance and the police. It wouldn't make any difference to Nick but it seemed important to us. So we waited with him, or at least in the canteen – partly because it was easier than saying our goodbyes and leaving him, partly because when the police got here they'd need to talk to us.

We didn't anticipate any difficulty with the police. The facts were clear enough: Nick had died because, in the throes of fever, he had tried to find his way in darkness and driving rain across a marsh that was treacherous by daylight. But the police would want statements as to his physical and mental state before the accident, and they'd want to be sure we had made all reasonable provision for his welfare after he fell ill.

Despite my grief I believed we had done all a reasonable man would have thought necessary to keep Nick safe. We had brought him ashore as soon as possible after his illness became a cause for concern. We had put him into the care of a doctor, in a well-equipped clinic, where he was treated appropriately as per his symptoms. He had been sleeping in a double room with Dr Rodway a wall away on one side and me on the other. As soon as he was missed we had instigated a comprehensive search. The tragedy had happened despite, not because of, our actions.

Though we hardly talked, sitting instead in a silence occasionally broken by the clatter of cups, we were all anxious to get the police interviews out of the way. Once John slammed the palms of his hands flat on the table in a startling explosion of sound and demanded, 'Where *are* they? What's keeping them? Don't they care that someone *died* here?'

Costigian was hunched over the table, the broad shoulders more bear-like than usual. Quietly, reasonably, he said, 'Sometimes it comes down not to what's important but to what's urgent. Someone who needs their help takes priority over someone who can't benefit. All they have to do here is paperwork.'

John's eyes stabbed at him, bitter and offended. 'Is that all this means to you – paperwork? Statistics?' His voice shook.

Marion folded her hand over his on the table top in a gesture of comfort and restraint that was somehow surprising in a civil servant. It was the sort of touching that good doctors learn not to be afraid of. The same quiet reassurance was in her voice. 'He's right, John. There's nothing the police can do here but tidy up. There's no crime to investigate, no evidence to collect, no villain to track down. There's no hurry now. Everyone pulled out all the stops when time mattered, but it doesn't matter any longer. It doesn't matter if we have to wait all day. Time can't hurt Nick now.'

John let his head sink on his chest and his body shuddered. Marion's hand held his, absorbing some of his pain.

Terry Hollis, who'd been as shocked as anyone by what had happened, was slowly reverting to type. He growled, 'It's not Nick who's being kept hanging round, though, is it?'

Chase stepped in quickly to avoid the misery around the table turning to anger. 'Come on, guys, let's hold it together. Getting ratty with one another isn't going to help. Let's just concentrate on getting through the next couple of hours. I'll go see if there's any sign of the police yet.'

Which left Hollis nominally in charge, and he was one of those men who never met a situation so irremediably awful that he couldn't make it worse. Now he fixed Marion with a jaundiced eye and said, 'What makes you such an authority on police procedure, anyway?'

A second before she told him, I knew. I understood her skill in crisis management. I understood her physical fitness. I could even hazard a guess about her dislike of Costigian. It had nothing to do with being here or anything that had passed between them in the last four days. They had met before. They were, after all, in the same business.

'I'm an inspector with the Metropolitan Police,' she said.

Hollis looked as if he'd bitten into an apple and found half a worm. 'You're a civil servant,' he said accusingly. 'It says so on your form.'

'I *am* a civil servant,' she agreed. 'My field of service is the Metropolitan Police. And the reason I'm cagey on booking forms is that if you write "Police", either there are no vacancies or you spend your holiday avoiding someone with a handcuff fetish.'

It was cards-on-the-table time. Costigian said, 'She's right. I have a lot of trouble with oversexed blondes with a handcuff fetish.'

Hollis stared. 'You too?'

'Royal Canadian Mounted Police. Only I'm taking a sabbatical.' He smiled at me and did not elaborate.

I said, 'You two know each other, don't you?'

Costigian said, 'Yes,' and Marion said, 'No.'

'Kind of,' said Costigian. 'We worked together one time.'

And then they'd come on holiday together, although Marion plainly felt about the Canadian as lambs feel about mint sauce? It didn't make sense. But neither of them was going to add anything more so I said, 'My husband's a policeman, if that counts.'

George Fox said, 'I was once arrested by a policeman,' and told us about the hitch-hiker with five wristwatches on each arm; and after that it was easier to talk than to remain silent, thinking of the still boy in the clinic, until Chase returned.

It didn't take a mind-reader to know he had bad news. George said, '*Now* what?'

'The phone lines are out. Last night's storm. They haven't been able to get through to the police yet.'

We'd been sitting there for ninety minutes. It was two hours since we had found Nick, three and a half since we had missed him. Now Chase was telling us the police knew nothing about it?

'Have you tried your mobile?'

He regarded me with restraint. 'Of course I've tried my mobile. Still no signal.' He tried again as we watched, but all he got was an odd little static display.

'Something's blocking it,' said Costigian.

I frowned. 'What sort of something?' But he only shrugged.

I was aware of a strange sensation, and the best way I can describe it is: imagine standing on a stepladder in an earthquake. At first you assume that it's you that's wobbling. Then you wonder if the ladder's rickety, and that's more unsettling. Finally you realize that you're steady and the ladder is sound and it's the earth that's shaking; and that rocks you to your foundations.

From the moment we had turned up here, clad in mud and exhaustion, and begged the use of their showers we'd looked on Growth Industries as a kind of Big Brother: not the kind that watches – the kind that watches over. We'd felt better for having them near. We knew that if things got too tough they were our way out. And when we'd needed help in a hurry they hadn't failed us. If Nick had come safely through his adventure, it would have been thanks to GI: to their doctor's care and the effort put into finding him by just about everybody at the plant.

Now the earth had shaken, and what I'd believed to be a firm point at the centre of an unstable world, the island in the bog, was suddenly awash. The phones were out? This was a multimillion-pound complex, not a line-shack. We weren't twenty miles from a good-sized town. And while it had been a wet and windy night, it wasn't the sort of weather that roots out telegraph poles. So why would the phones fail now? Only because we needed them so desperately?

Or was I losing touch with reality? Phone lines do occasionally fail. Everything fails occasionally. It was certainly a bad moment to choose, but such is life. You never lose your umbrella on a dry day.

For a long time no one spoke. I wasn't sure if my companions shared my unease or simply had nothing to say.

Finally George said, 'We could phone from The Wake.'

Chase shook his head. 'I suggested that. Apparently the line goes through here to the village. If we're cut off, they must be too.'

Marion took control. 'Well, we have to report what's happened somehow. We can't just wait for the phone to be reconnected, and God knows when mobiles will work again. I'll borrow a vehicle. George, will you go? I think I should stay here, and I think Tom should. Drive up the road until you find a phone that works, put through a 999 call and then come back. All right?'

George's sandy head inclined in a nod.

She turned to Chase. 'Who's in charge of the plant?'

'The chief executive isn't here. But the company secretary is – Ernest Wilson. I'll show you to his office.' They went out together.

I started to say, 'Someone must have called him . . .' But that meant the phones had gone down in that narrow band of time between Nick going missing and his body being brought back here. 'Maybe he's been here all night. I bumped into him yesterday evening outside Rodway's office. Maybe he worked late.'

George stared at me in frank disbelief. But it didn't strike me as unreasonable. 'This place is a long drive from anywhere he'd want to live. Maybe he stayed over rather than drive an hour each way for a couple of hours' sleep.' Rodway had a room here he could use, perhaps the company secretary did too. That had to be the explanation. A company like GI wouldn't have cut its own phone lines to avoid reporting the accidental death of a schoolboy.

Five minutes later Marion was back, with a curiously ambivalent expression and no car keys. 'They're getting the Land Rover ready. It'll be a little while yet.'

I had my mouth open to protest when I caught her eye, flashing me a warning. So I shut it again.

George hadn't caught the look. His habitual cool gave way to a small explosion of impatience. 'Never mind getting it ready! I'll take it with the mud still on it.'

This time she made sure she had his attention. Almost as

if she was afraid we might be overheard. 'There's a problem under the bonnet. I'm told they'll have it sorted any time.'

George looked as if he was going to say something more, then thought better of it.

At that point Marion took herself off to the Ladies. It was a signal that would have been picked up by any other woman. I waited a minute, then got up and followed her.

Almost, she grabbed me by the lapel as I went through the door. 'I don't know what's going on here but something is. George is right: Land Rovers don't go US because of a bit of mud, and anyway there must be other vehicles about the place. Wilson for one doesn't come and go in the company bus. He's stalling us, and I don't know why, but I do know we're not waiting any longer.'

'Did you tell him that?'

She shook the cap of red hair briskly. 'He knows I'm a police officer. If he's prepared to lie to me, (a) he must have a good reason, and (b) he must have decided what to do if I don't buy it. He isn't going to produce the Land Rover – he's going to make damn sure we can't get hold of anything else either. So I let him think I was resigned to waiting.'

I considered. 'Whereas in fact . . . ?'

She gave a quick tense grin. 'You'll be looking for a phone that's working and I'll be looking for transport.'

'What's our excuse for leaving the canteen?'

'I'm not feeling very well,' she said. It may have been true. 'You're taking me to the clinic to put my feet up.'

I nodded. If he was a gentleman at all, Wilson would not keep checking a lady's bed to make sure she was in it. 'I have a suggestion, but you won't like it.'

The auburn brows came together in a wary frown. 'What?'

'Get Costigian in on this. Someone needs to know what we're up to, if only to head off trouble.'

'George . . .'

'Costigian's cleverer than George, and sneakier, and if need be he'll flatten Wilson or anyone else who tries to put GI's interests ahead of ours while George is still wondering if violence is justified. He's a cop too, Marion. I know you don't like him, but I think we need him.'

She bit her lip. The green eyes were smoky, indecisive. 'It's not a question of liking him. I don't know if we can trust him. He makes bad decisions.'

It was the thing between them, which neither of them had spoken of. I said, 'Is that what happened, when you worked together? He let you down?'

'He . . .' Then she shook her head again. 'There isn't time. All right – if you get a chance, tell Costigian what we're doing. No one else. Tell him to do nothing until he hears from me. Now if you'll stand back,' she added, looking for hard edges to avoid, 'I'm going to faint.'

III

Third Dimension

Nine

I asked Costigian to help me take Marion to the clinic. I hoped no one would think it odd that I chose the man with the injured shoulder and the last man in the building to whom Marion would have turned for aid. But it was becoming important to get things done and I couldn't waste time dropping casual hints. So I asked Costigian, and he rose without a murmur and offered Marion his better arm.

As soon as we were out of sight she returned it, much as you might give a dead fish back to a cat. 'All right, this is what we're doing.' In a couple of sentences she sprinted over the ground she and I had already covered.

Costigian nodded slowly. 'What about the doctor?'

Marion looked at me, but I didn't know what he meant either. He explained. 'He's going to notice if you're supposed to be in his clinic and aren't. Are you going to ask him to keep quiet? If he thinks you're up to no good, he'll call Wilson as soon as you leave.'

He was right. Rodway had no reason to mistrust his employers whereas he could be forgiven for doubting us. Every time we met we were in some kind of trouble. 'Suppose I keep him talking?' I suggested.

'OK,' agreed Marion. 'Give me fifteen minutes, then go back to the canteen. I'll find a vehicle and collect everyone there. We'll argue about whether it's taking and driving away at the nearest police station.'

'I'll find you a vehicle,' promised Costigian. 'You look for that phone – there has to be a live one somewhere. I don't believe that the line waited till tonight to come down, and the company secretary just happened to be burning the midnight oil when it did.'

77

I said, 'What do you believe?'

'They're covering something up. Probably it's nothing to do with Nick, but they don't want the police here, not right now. They're stalling us until they can get their act together. That's what Wilson's doing in his office: papering over whatever it is they don't want anyone outside the company to know about. Once he's got it sorted, in half an hour or an hour or three hours from now, suddenly the phones will be back and the problem with the Land Rover will be solved, and they'll fall over themselves to do whatever we want – call the police, drive us there, whatever.'

'If that's all,' I murmured, 'perhaps we should go along with it. I mean, what's another hour? If it's nothing to do with us, why risk a confrontation? We can tell the police what we suspect when they finally get here.'

Costigian said with absolute conviction, 'By then there'll be nothing for them to see.'

I appealed to Marion. 'But how much does it matter? GI isn't responsible for what happened to Nick. That was sheer bad luck. How much does it matter if Wilson's fiddling his VAT?'

For a moment she seemed to waver; then she sighed. 'I'm a police officer – if I think a crime has been committed, I can't ignore it because it's a rotten bloody time. Maybe it's not a very big crime, but maybe it is. If they're hiding something, I have a duty to try and find out what. But I'll understand if you'd rather not be involved. It could get unpleasant. Well, that's what I'm paid for. You could even say he' – she indicated the Canadian with an off-handed thumb – 'has an obligation to law enforcement. But you haven't. If you want to wait in the canteen, that's fine.'

If there's one thing we short people cannot abide it's being made to feel small. I said with great dignity, 'Of course I'll help.'

She smiled. 'Then you keep Rodway off our backs, I'll look for a phone, Costigian'll get us some transport and we'll meet back at the canteen in fifteen minutes.'

I tried his office first. The light was on but he wasn't there, or in his own room. I found him in the room where the boys had been sleeping, now a temporary mortuary. He had the sheet drawn back from Nick's face and was looking at him with that mixture of pity, puzzlement and self-recrimination that every doctor feels contemplating a body that all his instincts tell him should still be a patient.

Patients die all the time: it's the nature of the job. But mostly their deaths are inevitable. Age or illness or injury have reduced them to a state inconsistent with continued life. Some of them have a chance, but it's not a good one and though you do everything you can to improve the odds, it comes as no surprise when, on a last throw of the dice, they lose.

But when you lose a patient who didn't seem to be in any danger, who seemed to be getting better, that's hard. You go over and over everything you did, everything you decided not to do. You must have made a mistake or he'd still be alive. He put himself in your hands, trusted you to make him well, and now he's lying under a white sheet and his dead face is full of questions for which you have no answers.

Donald Rodway was looking down at the body of a boy who should have had sixty years ahead of him, who'd had a nasty bout of flu and might have missed a week of his holiday, who hadn't even been sick enough to take to hospital, but who had died. He didn't know what he should have done differently but he blamed himself. He was trying to apologize.

I said gently, 'There was no way you could have foreseen this, you know.'

He didn't look round. 'He was my patient.' His voice was thick, sorrow bulking out the accent. 'He was in my care, and he died. If I'd been more careful; if I'd *watched* him . . .'

'What happened was an accident, Donald. You did everything anyone would have considered necessary.'

'But he's still dead.'

'People do die. Despite our best efforts, people do still die. You know that. You save some of them – most of the ones who can be saved. You have to be content with that. You're a doctor – a good, careful doctor doing his best. God is someone else.'

'That's the truth.' He sighed, unloading some of the grief in the relief of talking. 'Yesterday it seemed terribly important to establish what this marsh fever is. Now the autopsy will tell us and it hardly seems to matter at all.'

'It does matter. Because one day another kid on a survival course, or a bird-watcher, or one of your pipe-tappers is going to get it as badly as Nick did. And then the fact that you know what it is and how to treat it will stop him wandering off into a bog-hole. Medical textbooks are the boneyards of dead patients but the salvation of new ones. It's not a bad legacy, the seeds of someone else's survival.'

Carefully, tenderly, he replaced the sheet. 'I'm sorry – were you looking for me?' His eyes changed abruptly. 'Has someone else gone down with it?'

I couldn't tell him now that Marion was unwell – he'd insist on examining her. So I improvised. 'I was thinking. Maybe there's something in your files that would explain all this. I mean, the plant's been here twenty-five years – there must have been cases of marsh fever among the staff. Even at the rate of one or two a year, there might have been enough to make a pattern. If we go through the clinic records we might start to understand how this thing works – when it strikes, who's vulnerable. If the clues are scattered through your files, finding them is the one useful thing we can be doing while we wait for British Telecom to reconnect us to the outside world.'

Even within the confines of our small group, marsh fever had shown itself in forms as trivial as a bit of a headache and a runny nose and as serious as toxic shock. To be sure of spotting every case we had to consider every reported illness that fitted between those parameters. It was going to take longer than fifteen minutes.

That brought me up short. Already I was running out of time. I had to get back to the canteen. Any delay could be fatal to our plan. If Wilson really didn't want us to leave yet, he had enough security men and brawny pipe-tappers to stop us. 'I need caffeine. Can I bring you one?'

He nodded absently. 'Milk, no sugar.' And I left him there, wading through files that represented hours of work, waiting for the coffee I had no intention of bringing. I hoped by the time he missed me I'd be halfway to King's Lynn.

Marion and I arrived at the canteen together. 'Any luck?'

She shook her head. 'Nobody's getting a mobile signal, and all the land lines I tried were dead.'

'Costigian?'

'Haven't seen him.'

We went inside. Chase looked up, pleased to see Marion back on her feet. 'Feeling better?'

'Yes, thanks.' But her manner was distracted, her attention occupied in counting heads. Only Costigian's was missing.

Chase said, 'Is he going down with this thing too?' He was a worried man. Of course, he had reason to be. What had happened was no more his fault than Rodway's, but there was no escaping the fact that if his school prize had been tickets for a London theatre, Nick Baker would have been alive now.

Then we heard the quick tread of boots in the corridor and Costigian threw open the canteen door. He nodded at Marion.

'Right,' she said tersely. 'We've got transport and we're leaving. Keep together, keep the noise down and keep moving.' Such was her authority that the men were on their feet and filing through the door before anyone thought to question her.

Costigian took the lead. We followed him a back way of service corridors and storage areas, past a tank like a great fermentation vat painted with a figure '5', then through one more door and the day was waiting for us outside.

It was still early morning: the new shift wouldn't be here for an hour yet, but we'd been awake since two thirty and to us it seemed like high noon. Squinting against the daylight we tailed Costigian round a corner of the plant into a kind of blind pocket between the fourth and fifth brick lean-tos where our transport awaited.

It was a Transit van. A purist might have argued that it was the remains of a Transit van, that in a decent society it would have been taken into the bog at midnight and buried in an unmarked grave. But someone had thought it might be useful for spare parts. So it had sat gently mouldering, waiting to be cannibalized, unnoticed and maybe even unseen in this blind alley behind the plant, for months if not years.

It seemed unlikely to move again, except at the end of a strong rope. I looked at Costigian. 'Er . . .'

One of the doors was seized when we tried to open it. Another fell off.

'Will it go?'

He threw me an impatient glance. 'Of course it'll go. It's got everything it needs to go – I checked. I'd have polished the windshield for you, Clio, only by then I was running out of time.'

Marion paused from herding her little flock on board. 'Don't talk about it. Do it.'

It almost didn't start. He got some deep abdominal rumblings out of it, some bronchial whirrings and a couple of half-choked coughs; then it breathed out tinnily and I thought it had died. Costigian looked up, his teeth showing in a snarl.

Finally the spark caught. Marion, who had taken the wheel, played delicately with the accelerator, coaxing the engine to life. From the firm conviction that he was mad, a seed of hope was growing in me that the Canadian could get this apology for a vehicle to carry us across the marsh to safety.

But it sounded like an outboard motor in a bucket: if there was anything left of the silencer, it could only be the retaining bolts. We wouldn't go unnoticed for much longer. Costigian slammed the bonnet and jumped aboard, and immediately Marion had the van under way, proceeding determinedly towards the gate.

Chase observed to me, quite quietly, 'I'm not sure I know what's going on here.'

'None of us does,' I assured him. 'We think there's something going on that we're not supposed to know about; we don't know what it is, and we don't want to hang around while somebody decides whether or not to tell us.' If he was any the wiser for my explanation, it didn't show.

'Look. You know Marion's a police inspector?' He nodded.

'Hold on to that thought. Everything that happens from now on is her responsibility.' I might as well have said *fault*: it was what I meant.

The gate was open, but as we approached, the guard came out of his hut and, puzzled, stood blocking our way. It was full daylight, peering into the van he had no difficulty recognizing us. He also recognized the Transit. 'Isn't that . . . ?'

'Yes,' Marion said briskly. 'I am an inspector of the Metropolitan Police: I have borrowed this vehicle to take these people to the nearest police station. It will then be returned.'

The gateman wasn't sure he should let us leave with company property. 'Have you got a chit?'

'No, I haven't got a chit,' snapped Marion. 'I've got a warrant card instead. It authorizes me to borrow this van, Sir Emlyn's limo and your bicycle too if I need them. Now get out of the way.'

A lot of taxpayers' money had gone into teaching her the manner of command so that when she said 'Jump', people would jump. Not a penny had been wasted. The man moved. But he shouted after us, 'I'll have to report this!'

But by then we were in the clear. The causeway opened before us and there was nothing to stop us driving until we hit civilization. Then we'd find out what was going on at Growth Industries. Or maybe we'd find out that nothing was, that it really was just a combination of odd coincidences, in which case we'd have some apologies to make.

I looked back at the red-brick complex with the marsh closing round it and a pang of guilt caught me under the ribs. I'd left Nick alone in a cold room, in an alien place, with people who didn't know him and had no reason to care if he was alive or dead. He deserved better. If one of us had sat with him last night he'd have been alive now. I understood why Marion had to leave, but I should have stayed with him.

I had my mouth open to ask her to let me out when I saw the ATVs. 'Marion.'

She checked her mirror. 'I've got them.'

Everyone was looking back now. Chase said reasonably, 'We'd better stop and find out what they want.'

'Like hell,' grunted Marion, pumping extra revs out of the engine and taking up a position on the crown of the road.

But the ATVs didn't have to stay on the road. They were designed to cross trackless marsh. Just a few hours ago I had been profoundly grateful for that. But now, as they swung off the causeway, bouncing pneumatically, I had the sick sensation of being the last wagon in the train when the Indians come racing up the trail. I don't know what I was expecting. More than a message – that wouldn't take eight men on four vehicles – but less than a massacre. Yet the threat was real. The ATVs weren't there to see us safe across the marsh: they'd been sent to stop us.

Marion kept her foot down, nursing the van towards whatever top speed it was capable of, its well-worn tyres sliding in the mud. But the outcome was never in doubt. On an open road we might have made a match of it, but not here. The ATVs overhauled us and skidded to a halt, chevron-shaped, blocking the road.

Crouching in the aisle Costigian murmured, 'You could go through them.'

Marion didn't spare him a glance. 'I'm not prepared to do murder!' The Transit stopped a van's length from the ATVs.

Four of the men came to meet us. They seemed to think they'd be enough to cope with the likes of us and – looking at their black leathers and helmets, then looking at us – I was inclined to agree. They split up, placing themselves by the Transit's doors.

Marion wound her window down a few inches. 'Is there a problem?'

The men were wearing full-face motorcycle helmets with tinted visors. The one at Marion's door pushed his visor halfway up, his eyes remaining hidden behind the dark perspex. 'That van belongs to Growth Industries.'

'Of course. I'm a police officer, I'm taking these people to a police station.'

Beneath the visor his lips sketched a smile. A gauntleted hand opened the driver's door. 'I'm sorry, Constable . . .'

'Inspector,' she corrected him, still very calmly.

'Sorry, Inspector. But I have instructions to take you back to the plant so this can be cleared up.'

She gave him her most autocratic frown – the one they test you on at your inspector's board. 'I've told you what to do: move those bikes. If you want to safeguard this valuable piece of company property you can come with us. Climb aboard, there's room at the back.'

He seemed to consider it. Then he reached into the cab and – not violently but with enough force to overcome any resistance – pulled Marion out and down the side of the vehicle. 'No, darling – you sit in the back and I'll drive.'

It was one of those crossroads moments. Until then there had been a chance that it really was just a misunderstanding – that we had misread GI's motives and they had misconstrued our response; that the whole thing could be resolved with nothing worse than red faces at the nearest police station. That option passed when a company employee refused to comply with a lawful instruction from someone he knew to be a police officer. This wasn't about the van: it would have been the same if we'd tried to walk out. Someone at GI had decided we couldn't be allowed to leave, and had done so in the full knowledge that he had no legal defence.

George opened the passenger door and climbed down. 'Don't squabble – you can have my seat.' His voice was so amiable no one tried to stop him. 'I'll ride pillion on one of the bikes.'

A jolt of understanding hit me. If he could grab an ATV there was no reason to suppose the others could overtake him. All he needed was a few seconds to tip one of the riders into a handy sink-hole and be on his way. I found Costigian's eyes on me and saw he'd understood too. But I didn't see what we could do to help.

Costigian said loudly, 'Of course they're not going to rape her, you crazy bitch.'

I stared at him, opened my mouth, realized what he was doing, closed it, decided it was worth a try, opened it again and started squealing.

I've never been an hysterical woman. Medical school discourages hysteria on principle: there's enough chaos in the average A&E department without the doctors tearing their hair. But I'd seen enough of it down the years to know how distracting a woman's screaming can be. So I hammed it up for all I was worth. I took a deep breath and cried, 'No – no – please, somebody, help!'

My companions stared as if they thought I'd been at the glue. I shrieked, 'Are you men or mice?' and every other cliché I could think of, including 'The end is nigh' and 'Do not pull the chain while the carriage is stationary.' And it worked. Every eye was glued to this screeching harpy. For just a moment everything else was forgotten.

Then Costigian kicked the back door out of the Transit, sending the man stationed there flying, and Marion kneed her assailant somewhere delicate. George, finding himself with no one watching him and almost no one near him, reached for the nearest rider and hauled him off backwards. He threw a long leg over the saddle, kicked the machine into gear and twisted up the throttle. The ATV reared like a start-led horse; he threw his weight forward to bring it down and then he was accelerating, the big tyres spitting mud.

He almost made it. It was just bad luck that the bikes had pulled up facing the van. To make his getaway, first he had to turn. It took a moment too long. The shock-effect of our diversion wore off. The security men realized what was happening and moved to stop it. The last rider still in the saddle rammed his machine forward as George tried to turn, the wheels locking with a horrible rubber squeal. Another snatched up a wheel-brace. Not many motorists carry the toolkit on the outside of the vehicle, so he'd kept it handy for use as a weapon.

He came up on George's blind side. All the same, something warned him – perhaps the fresh urgency of our shouting, perhaps that sixth sense for imminent danger – because at the last possible moment he ducked.

But it was already too late. The iron bar glanced viciously across the back of his skull and down his shoulder. George's head rocked back and his long body arched. Then all the strength ran out of him and he tumbled bonelessly out of sight among the ATVs.

Ten

Whatever it was – sight, sound or sixth sense – that made George turn, it saved his life. The bar that must otherwise have crushed his skull glanced past and came down on his shoulder instead. His collarbone shattered under the impact: surgery on it would be like doing a jigsaw puzzle. But a comparable head injury would have killed him.

Hollis helped Costigian carry him to the van and I had them lay him carefully on the floor, padding it soft with borrowed clothing. Before I had finished examining him he was on his way back, pain reaching down through the darkness. He moaned and his eyes flickered open. But they remained vacant, unfocused, and after a moment they fell shut again. He was close but he wasn't awake yet.

'We have to take him to a hospital.' My voice was flat, emotionless. I knew it wasn't going to happen.

The man with his visor up, still bent slightly in the middle, grunted, 'Dr Rodway'll take care of him.'

Chase, who had said almost nothing since we left the canteen, looked from George to me to the man in the helmet. He was down to his T-shirt: the two sweaters he'd been wearing had gone to cushion George's ride. He said, 'I'm responsible for this man's safety. If Dr Marsh says he should be in hospital, that's where I'm taking him.'

The guard sighed. 'Don't make this more difficult, Tom. I've got my orders. I don't understand this any more than you do, but I know who pays my wages. You might remember that GI's been a good friend to you, too.'

Chase's jaw came up and his eyes kindled. 'Orders? You had *orders* to attack my people with iron bars? I don't know what the hell you think you're doing, Gallagher, but if you're expecting me to cover for you, you'll do time.'

Gallagher said stiffly, 'I'm doing my job. If you want an explanation, ask Mr Wilson. The sooner we get back to the plant, the sooner he can put you in the picture and the sooner Dr Rodway can fix up your client. All right?'

Chase's lip curled with bridled anger. 'You're refusing to let me take an injured man to hospital? In spite of Dr Marsh's opinion and Inspector Fletcher's instructions?'

'That's right. Now climb aboard, we're going back.'

We could have argued some more. There seemed no point. There were eight of them, all well-built lads. There were eight of us too, but two of us were women, one was unconscious, John was still obviously unwell and most of us were under par to some extent. We could delay the outcome, we couldn't alter it.

'OK,' Costigian agreed suddenly. 'Come on, guys, let's find out what this is all about. You want to drive?' he asked Gallagher as the man herded us firmly back aboard the van.

In order to drive Gallagher took off his helmet. After trying to argue with a tinted visor his face came as a shock: round, ruddy, framed by fairish hair and featuring a ginger moustache. An ordinary, pleasant, unremarkable face, not one you'd associate with vicious attacks on innocent people.

The causeway was narrow but a careful nine-point turn had us facing back towards GI. The ATVs followed in a cautious procession. Soon the red-brick walls of the plant began to climb again out of the marsh.

As we came up to the turn-off, Costigian, crouching in the aisle behind the driver's left shoulder, said reasonably, 'Why don't you take us into Graveleigh instead? We'll sort it out from there.'

'Sorry,' said Gallagher shortly.

Costigian nodded. 'I reckoned you'd say that.' He said to Marion, in the front passenger seat, 'Take the wheel, will you?' Then laying powerful hands on the startled driver's shoulders he hauled him over the back of his seat into the aisle.

As soon as I realized what he was doing I moved to shield George from flying extremities. The back of a Transit van is not the ideal venue for an all-in wrestling match. Between protecting George and protecting myself I missed some of the details, but by the time Marion had wriggled past the gear-stick Costigian had subdued his man, turned him on his face, secured his hands with a bit of twine from the floor of the van and sat on him.

'Base Camp?' asked Marion tersely, and Costigian replied, 'Graveleigh. See if their phones are working.'

His actions had surprised our people at least as much as the man with the ginger moustache. On both sides of the aisle they had come out of their seats, jostling to see what was going on. Chase waved them back, as calm in this real crisis as in those he made his living simulating. 'Sit down, everyone, and let's work out what we do next.'

Gallagher looked up at him, his face pink with exertion. 'You get this maniac off me and come back to the plant, that's what you do! What do you think this is, the Wild West? You people are crazy!'

'*We're* crazy?' echoed Costigian. 'Hey, fella, nobody went for you with a tyre-iron.'

'You're stealing GI property! I'm security – that makes it my job to stop you.'

'You don't even *think* that justifies what you've done.'

We were at the turn-off, Marion's gaze darting between the plant, the road ahead and the mirror. The ATVs were still behind us and there was no indication that they realized there'd been a change of plan until she put her foot hard on the accelerator and the van lurched forward like an elderly carthorse at Aintree. I pinned George to the floor and watched through the back window.

For a moment the ATVs didn't react. Then they too throttled hard, exhausts belching, riders bouncing as the big tyres met the ruts. But they didn't try to pass us. Of course, there wasn't the same need as when we had been heading for civilization. Perhaps they knew our hopes were futile. Perhaps they thought if they herded us into Graveleigh, that was as good as having us locked up. So they made no great effort to close the small gap that had opened between us. But I never believed they were letting us go.

George blinked up at me from the floor. At last there was

some intelligence in his eyes. He whispered, 'Somebody hit me.'

Relief made me smile. 'I know they did, George.'

'What's the damage?'

I told him. 'It's going to hurt when we move you, I'm afraid. But when we get to The Wake I'll strap it up. That should help.'

'Oh good,' he said without much enthusiasm.

Costigian was leaning over us. 'Can he walk?'

'With a little help from his friends.' But unless his friends didn't care how much they hurt him it would take a little time, and I didn't relish the prospect of moving him from the van to The Wake with the pursuit roaring up the street behind us.

Costigian nodded. Over his shoulder to Marion he said, 'Let me out when you reach the first houses. I'll hold them off while you get inside.'

I stared at him. It was seven to one: I doubted if even the Mounties favoured odds like that. '*How?*'

He grinned fiercely and patted his hostage on the head. 'With a little help from *my* friend.'

'Watch out for the one who hits people,' said George, closing his eyes again.

The low mound that was The Island heaved itself out of the marsh and the track turned into a cobbled street. There were no outlying cottages where the wasteland turned by degrees into village: in Graveleigh the cottages needed one another's support to withstand the gales. They huddled together for support, warmth and company like old men on a park bench, their bony shoulders angular, their grizzled heads held low.

Marion braked, I opened the back door and Costigian stepped carefully over George. So did Gallagher, which was oddly touching. Hollis rose from his seat. 'I'll come with you.' I remembered him climbing that wall, the sheer pleasure with which he pitted his strength against danger, and thought I understood.

At the little alley leading down to the harbour Marion backed in, the Transit stopping it as a cork stops a bottle.

She leapt down and began hammering on the door of The Wake. I was amazed it was shut: it seemed to suggest that the old man in the corner had a home to go to. Or maybe it was him that shut it, to avoid being roused too early by the throngs of bustling Graveleigh.

I hoped Marion would find a phone that was still working. I hoped Costigian and Hollis could hold off the pursuit until we got inside. But there was nothing I could do on either score, so I concentrated on doing what I was better qualified than anyone else there to do: helping George.

Chase held him while I used my sweater – no, Nick's, that I'd never got round to returning – to tie his left arm to his side. Then we eased his feet to the ground, Chase took his weight and we walked him slowly into The Wake.

Saul Penny was at the phone with Marion. I knew from her face it was bad news. 'Dead?'

'Dead,' she nodded. Her voice was flat but we both knew what it meant: that we still had no way of communicating our situation to the outside world. We were as much prisoners here as we had been in the GI canteen.

'Do you know when it went out?'

Saul's huge shoulders shrugged up to his shaggy head. 'It was working half an hour ago – I heard it ping.' That was it going down. We did the sums, Marion and I, came up with the same answer: GI had disconnected the switchboard and jammed the mobile signals – possibly by scrubbing out the number 5 condenser, whatever the hell that meant – hours before, when they'd realized we'd want to call the police; but they'd cut the lines only after we left the plant. There had been nothing to prevent them reporting Nick's death when they should have done.

I couldn't deal with the implications of that, and with Marion there I didn't have to. She had the skill, the training and the authority to decide our course of action. What I was trained in was bandaging. Saul found me what I needed, including painkillers from his mother's cabinet that would take the edge off George's hurts. He was glad when I finished, but by then the black tide of concussion had ebbed, leaving him sore but essentially himself.

Chase was watching with concern, wondering how much of what had happened was his fault. I didn't think any of it was, but that didn't alter the fact that if he'd stayed with GI security instead of opening the Graveleigh School of Adventure, Nick and George would both be fine. I said quietly, 'No one blames you for this.'

He started as if I'd read his mind. He began to say something, changed his mind and backed towards the door. 'I'll go see how Costigian's making out . . .'

He hadn't far to go. He opened the door that we'd locked behind us and Costigian stumbled in as if he'd been leaning on it. I thought for a moment that was all it was – that he'd stumbled. Then I saw the blood running over his hand.

Chase's eyes snapped up to meet the Canadian's. 'What happened? Where's Terry?'

'Terry,' Costigian said heavily, a slight breathiness in his voice, 'is on his way back to Growth Industries with his pal with the ginger whiskers, to tell Mr Wilson what we know, what we guess and what we're likely to do next. And to indent for a new Swiss Army knife, since he left the old one in me.'

It was a minor exaggeration forgivable in the circumstances. The blade had lodged not in his flesh but in the several layers of clothes he'd pulled on at three o'clock this morning when word had reached Base Camp about the missing boy. He had a ten-centimetre wound down the outside of his forearm, but it was clean and not deep and it hadn't stopped him from freeing the weapon himself and making a determined swipe with it in Hollis's direction. The blade hadn't got within half a metre but the intention had. Hollis had extended the world record for the backward standing leap by about fifty per cent; then he was running to meet the ATVs.

Gallagher had hesitated, reluctant to give best to a man who was outnumbered and already bloodied. But Hollis wasn't coming back and he couldn't be sure of taking the big man alone. So, making a point of not hurrying, he had swung himself on to the back of an ATV and headed for GI and fresh instructions. Costigian had watched until he was sure they were all going, Hollis included, then he came on to The Wake. By the time he got here he was aware that he was bleeding.

Lacking the proper facilities I decided against stitching it. Instead I bound his arm firmly, before sitting him down next to George and telling them to keep an eye on one another. Then I went to see why Marion was summoning me with jerks of her red head.

'We're getting out of here,' she said briskly. 'We can't go across the marsh – they hold the track – so we're going by sea. There's a fishing boat in the harbour and there's *Grainne*. You're the sailor, Clio – which is our best bet?'

I'd have given anything to be able to say that the century-old sailing boat could show a modern – or since this was Graveleigh, reasonably modern – trawler a clean pair of heels. But people's safety depended on this, my own not least. 'The fishing boat.'

'Can you handle it?'

I stared at Saul. 'You think I'll have to?'

His dark eyes were ashamed. 'This is Graveleigh, remember? – where they wouldn't piss on you if you were burning, where the priests and the Levites walk by on the other side of the road but the Samaritans walk clean over the top of you. Nobody here will lift a finger to help you.'

I didn't understand. 'You said no one from The Island worked for Growth Industries.'

'But they do live here, and the plant's a powerful neighbour. They won't stand with you against GI, not if your lives depend on it. They wouldn't for one of their own, let alone strangers. These are Islanders: they haven't much sense of civic duty.'

I bit back the disbelieving anger. 'Except you.'

His eyes fell and his twisted face managed a rueful smile. 'Oh yes, me. For what that's worth. I'm not scared of them. They've already done all they can to me.'

This wasn't the time to go into it. For now, however unreasonable, his hatred of the plant was a weapon in our hands and we hadn't so many we could afford to throw one away. I answered Marion's question. 'Yes, I can handle it. If we can break into the wheelhouse, and if you can hot-wire the engine for me.'

It's wonderful what they teach you at police college. 'Fine. Saul, we'll need some tools – hacksaw, crowbar, that sort of thing.' He nodded his maned head eagerly. 'Then let's do it.'

Given luck it would be the work of moments. If Marion and I could get aboard the *Keith and Mary* unobserved we could have her ready to leave as soon as the others joined us. We could be on our way while her skipper was still standing open-mouthed on the quay trying to remember the last time anything was stolen in Graveleigh.

That was the theory. Even if we were unlucky and the skipper was on board, Marion could try waving her warrant card again. If these people were scared to cross their neighbours for fear of unpleasantness, they weren't going to poke a police inspector in the eye. The likelihood was that they'd back off and let us get on with it. And once we were at sea it would take an armed patrol boat to stop us, and I didn't think even Ernest Wilson could have hidden one of those in his VAT return.

So, trying to look more like trippers than pirates, Marion and I secreted our blagging kit in a PVC shopping bag bearing the legend *'Publicans do it with their optics open'* and hurried down the alley towards the harbour.

Before we even got there the sound warned us what we would find. At the harbour wall we stopped, dropped our shopping with a clank and watched the *Keith and Mary* motor over the bar with *Grainne* nodding to a hawser behind.

'Buggery,' said Marion.

They weren't expecting us back at The Wake. Our urgent knocking brought no response; only at the sound of our voices did they unlock the door. We explained in a few words. No one made any reply, but you could hear the dull rumble of hearts falling into boots.

'Is there *any* other way out?' asked Marion.

Saul didn't answer immediately. Then he shook his head. 'No.'

'No other track across the marsh?' Even if we couldn't all

make it, someone might get through to raise the alarm.

'Maybe. But they'll be watching. No one on foot could stay ahead of those swamp-bikes.'

'Could we do it by night? If we could hold them off that long?'

'Suicide,' said Saul succinctly.

Chase was following the exchange intently. 'I'll try it. If they haven't overrun us by tonight, I'll have a go.'

Saul shook his head forcefully. 'People who've lived all their lives on The Island don't go into the marsh at night. It's a death-trap. You know that.'

Tom Chase's eyes blazed round the public bar of The Wake. 'And this isn't?' Bitterness ran through his voice like a steel thread. His partner's defection had been the final humiliation: anything he could do now to expiate that treachery he would do. 'If we can't get out, and we can't get a message out, we're all going to die here. After what's happened already, Wilson can't let us go.'

That was it, out in the open. He was right and all of us knew it, but somehow saying it aloud seemed to shut off a last line of retreat. There was no refuge for us now, even in innocence.

'All right,' Marion said, exhaling the words slowly, 'we're in deep shit, we may have to take desperate measures. But I'm not risking lives unless there's no alternative. There must be other boats. It's a harbour, for God's sake!'

'It *was* a harbour,' Saul corrected her, 'like Graveleigh *was* a village. Now Graveleigh's a place where old fishermen come to die, and the harbour's where old boats do. There's a couple of rowing boats still in use, but everything else you can see there isn't afloat, it's sitting on the bottom. When the tide's in, half of them disappear entirely.'

Like Chase and his track across the marsh, I thought I could make it by rowing boat. But the problems were much the same. By day I would be totally exposed. By night I'd be safer on the sea than Chase would be in the marsh, but I couldn't beat the wind and tide any more than *Grainne* had been able to. Either I would be driven back on to this unfriendly shore or I'd find myself rowing like hell and still in the same spot when the sun came up.

Added to which, whether it was a lone rower or a lone runner going for help, the departure of someone fit enough to try it would leave the rest of the group less able to deal with whatever GI thought up next. My instinct was that we should stay together, that splitting up would play into the hands of our enemy. What we needed was a way of getting everyone away, or else holding out until we should be missed.

That might be three days yet. We weren't due to leave here until Saturday morning; no one would miss us until Saturday night and it would be Sunday or later before anyone came looking. They would find our gear and no indication of where we'd gone, and would hang around another half-day waiting for someone to show up before finally reporting us missing. Unless we were very lucky we had three full days to wait for relief. Unless we were quite lucky we could have longer than that.

We had no weapons; some of us were sick, some were hurt; on top of that we had Saul and his mother to consider. We couldn't hold The Wake against the sort of assault GI's security corps could mount if this really had gone that far. It was a pub, not a Martello tower. Half a dozen determined men could overwhelm us. A dozen could occupy the entire village.

Saul said diffidently, 'There *is* another boat. I don't know if you could use her. She's not seaworthy, but ten miles up The Wash isn't an ocean voyage.'

Hope quickened my blood. 'Where is she?'

'In the river behind The Island, in a mud-berth. She could be dug out in an hour.'

'Who owns it?' asked Marion. 'Will we have to fight him for it?'

His jaw jutted proudly in its jungle of beard. 'She's mine.'

She was a Norfolk wherry. She must have been twenty metres long, and with her mast on the deck and the mud holding her hull in a close embrace she looked like one of those ship burials that make archaeologists drool. And she didn't look much younger. The planks of her deck were faded to an indeterminate colour like grey bones, yawning in wide cracks. The timbers of her hull had a dark greasiness that spoke of rot. A black canvas was stretched across her hold: I thought this tarpaulin had weathered rather better than the rest of the boat until I saw the yard still laced at one end and realized it was the sail. Her rigging was of hempen rope, which time and the sun had opened out and marsh birds had picked at for nesting material. What had once been tarred and hard was now pale and fuzzy, and the wooden blocks were cracked.

Some flaking paint clung round the low bow. It was possible to make out the name *Hereward* inscribed in Gothic letters.

Saul said hopefully, 'What do you think?'

My first impulse was to damn him for wasting our time at this critical moment. But when I saw the desperate longing in his eyes I knew it wasn't a joke. He thought there was a chance his boat could sail again. I made myself speak gently. 'How long has she been here?'

'Eight, nine years?' He hurried on: 'But she's sound enough. She's not leaking. If we got her into the river, she'd float.'

Maybe she would. But then she'd have to leave the river and go to sea. Even if her hull was sound, all her gear was rotten. There was no engine, and getting her mast up would be a major undertaking. As a means of escape we'd be better building a raft.

'Was she your dad's boat?'

'My grandfather's. He worked her till he retired. When he died I thought I could fix her up.' He shrugged, trying to make out that it didn't matter. 'I never had the money. To haul her out, re-rig her, do a proper job, would cost more than I'm worth. I'd sell The Wake, but who'd buy it? So *Hereward* rots here and I rot over there, and one day there'll be nothing left to show either of us ever existed.'

It hadn't been a joke but it had been a dream. He hadn't believed *Hereward* could sail again. He'd wanted her to, had wanted that moment of glory for both of them, but he hadn't thought it would happen. He looked up now and managed a wry smile. 'Maybe if we'd three months . . . ?'

I smiled too. 'It was a nice thought.' We went back before his crutches sank as far into the mud as his boat.

Eleven

A visitor was waiting at The Wake. I saw the car as soon as we turned off the path from the river. My heart thumped and I stopped Saul in mid-swing, one hand clutching his arm.

'That's Dr Rodway's car,' he said.

I should have known that: I'd ridden in it. Still, there was no guarantee that he was alone. We approached cautiously.

Chase met us at the door. 'They've sent a negotiator.' He seemed unimpressed by Rodway's credentials.

We walked into the middle of the conversation, but it wasn't difficult to pick up the threads. Rodway was trying to convince Marion that we'd overreacted, and Marion wanted to know what he considered an appropriate level of response when one of their men hit one of ours with an iron bar.

He apologized fulsomely for that, promised that the man responsible would be disciplined, but pointed out that the security men had been trying to recover stolen property and apprehend the thieves.

I couldn't stay silent any longer. 'Have you *seen* George's clavicle? That was a wheel-brace, and it only got his shoulder because he moved his head!'

Rodway blanched a little. 'That was unforgivable,' he admitted. 'Even if the chap was having his bike pinched at the time. What can I tell you? – Nobody wanted that to happen. People get carried away. If it comes to criminal charges, GI will accept its responsibilities and the man concerned will have to accept his. Come back with me to the plant and talk to Ernest Wilson about it. It's all been a terrible misunderstanding.

'All the company wanted was to help – when you were

fed up, when Nick was sick, when he went missing. It was damned bad luck that the phones went out when they did, but if you work in the middle of a bog it's the sort of thing that happens. We'll likely get back there now and find we've been reconnected. It was unfortunate, but I cannot understand why you think it's a conspiracy.'

Nothing in his voice, his face or the depths of his eyes called him a liar. He believed we were unbalanced by the shock of Nick's death, saw no reason why we couldn't return to the plant, trade apologies and leave. I said, 'Dr Rodway, I don't know what it is and maybe you don't either, but something is going on at Growth Industries which has nothing to do with fertilizer. Think about it. If it was just us over-reacting, why have I got two injured men, why was the causeway blockaded, and why have the only boats capable of sailing out of here just gone?'

He seemed genuinely to doubt my sanity. 'The fishing boats? They've gone fishing.'

'*Grainne* isn't a fishing boat. We brought her to Graveleigh. No one else had any business moving her.'

'Maybe she was in the way. Maybe her owner wanted her back. Maybe—'

'Maybe Wilson paid to have her towed away so we couldn't leave.'

'But . . .' I saw the idea finally gain a kind of hold in his eyes. His brow furrowed. '*Why?*'

'If I knew that, Donald,' I sighed, 'I'd be a wiser and possibly happier person.'

'Well – what are you going to do?'

'We're going to stay here and hope that the phones come on, or someone comes looking for us, or Wilson realizes he can't get away with this and calls the police himself. Or that maybe someone else does.'

He understood me well enough though he said nothing. His gaze dropped quickly and he backed towards the door. 'I'll tell Ernest what you said.'

'You do that,' nodded Marion.

But he hadn't quite gone. Reaching the car, he turned back on a sudden thought and said, 'This morning, when you left

100

me looking through the files, I found something. At least, I think I did.'

'The marsh fever?'

'I imagine so. The same symptoms as Nick's, right down to the delirium. It came on slower but it got bad enough in the end that there was no alternative but to ship him out of the marsh altogether.'

'One of the pipe-tappers, was it?' The maintenance crews undoubtedly had other, more formal titles but they'd always be pipe-tappers to me.

'No. It was my predecessor, Dr Burke. He left here this spring but he'd been sick and getting worse all winter.'

It was the first firm evidence that the illness could affect people who lived or worked around Graveleigh. 'Is there any indication what caused it?'

'Not in the files,' said Rodway. 'But I asked around and there's one thing. He's an ornithologist. He took this post specifically to study winter visitors in the marsh.'

Still thinking about that, I went back inside.

Costigian locked the door behind me. His expression was deeply sceptical. 'He won't help us. He hasn't the guts.'

I'd come to the same conclusion; it was only wishful thinking that made me argue. 'Maybe you're right. Maybe he'll sit on the fence as long as he can. But if anyone else gets hurt, maybe he'll feel he has to take sides. I want him to take ours.'

'We'll be in wooden boxes before he'll see a problem.'

Marion had other priorities. 'The boat. Can we use it?'

I glanced at Saul and Saul looked away. I shook my head. 'It would take too long. Even if we had the time, I don't know if it'd stay afloat.'

'God damn!' For a moment before she had them under control her frustration and fear were live things in the room with us, like a pair of savage dogs someone had carelessly let off the leash. Circumstances had projected her into a situation no amount of training could have prepared her for and we were all looking to her for leadership. The rest of us had only to worry about our own lives. Marion had to worry about hers and everyone else's as well.

Costigian said to no one in particular, 'So what we've got is a wreck of a truck that can only move on a road held by the opposition; phones that are being jammed by the opposition; a footpath that'll be watched by the opposition, except at night when anyone using it is going to end up in the bog; and a boat that might or might not sail if we had unlimited time, manpower and materials. Maybe I was wrong. Maybe Rodway *is* our best chance.'

Chase said quietly, 'If we're still here when it gets dark I'm going to try the path.'

The idea of him groping along an unmarked path through that wet wilderness in the dark was ice-water in my veins. 'Nick died because he strayed four feet off the causeway.'

'Nick was ill. He didn't know what he was doing. I do.'

Costigian said, 'They're going to be watching us. They'll expect us to try something. If Tom's going to try the marsh, we should give them something else to think about.'

'Like what?' The momentary despair had cleared from Marion's eyes and her mind was working again.

The big man shrugged. 'We could dig the boat out. It'll give them a laugh if nothing else. From then on they won't be watching us, they'll be watching the boat. Maybe Tom can slip away while there's still enough light on the marsh to keep him from making holes in it.'

I was reluctant to raise this. I thought I knew the answer, but if this thing ended badly I would always wonder if it had been necessary. 'Before we do anything else we ought to make quite sure we're on our own in this. If we could bully the village into helping us – if the chap who took the *Keith and Mary* away could be talked into bringing her back, for instance – there might be no need for anyone to take any more risks.'

I felt Saul's eyes and turned in time to catch the tail of his expression. I expected resentment that I hadn't taken his word on this, but it was shame. He felt about Graveleigh the way Chase felt about Hollis: tainted by a betrayal he had no power to prevent.

Marion agreed. 'If only so no one can say later that we didn't ask for help. You come with me, Clio. The rest of you, or those who can, go down to the boat and look as if you're doing something useful.'

There followed one of the most surreal half-hours of my life. It was a sequence straight from a dream. We walked up and down the single street, rapping on every door and peering through every window, and we couldn't find a living soul. The shop was locked up and the blinds pulled down. We saw curtains twitching at the windows ahead as we worked our way from house to house, but by the time we reached them the curtains were still and the houses silent. We knocked at doors and listened at letter boxes, but not a whisper of sound suggested there were people in Graveleigh apart from us.

Saul had said there were a couple of dozen people in the village. Even if it had taken a full crew to shift the boats, every second house should have been occupied. But by the time we were halfway up the street we were getting the message. We exchanged incredulous glances. There were maybe twenty people within earshot who knew we were in danger, who might be able to help us, and who wouldn't so much as acknowledge our presence.

They weren't even in the pay of Growth Industries. I could understand the men on the ATVs better than these people: at least they could say their loyalty had been bought. But these last remnants of the fenland community kept out of GI's way simply because it was easiest. The path of least resistance. They'd never take up cudgels against us; they'd never do anything they could be accused of in court. But not helping us wasn't a crime, particularly if they could claim they'd never known we needed help. If they all had their hearing aids tuned to the weather forecast at the very same time, who could be blamed for that?

I shivered, the dank of the marsh entering my soul. They weren't even afraid of what GI might do. The plant couldn't do anything more to them than they'd done to themselves: fossilized themselves, turned themselves to stone because of the inconvenient sensitivity of flesh.

And it was still bloody raining.

We finished hammering the doors. Marion stood in the

103

middle of the silent street and, turning slowly on her heel, glared balefully round the curtained windows. She raised her voice as they had taught her in crowd-control classes. 'All right. We'll do it without you. Or we'll fail and they'll kill us. The rest of the world will call it a tragic accident, but you'll know. You'll know you let seven people die rather than open your doors to them.

'Here's a thought to be going on with. If Growth Industries get away with killing us to protect their secret, it's only a matter of time before they start worrying about you. If they don't get away with it, the police'll want to talk to you; and if we survive, I will. Whatever happens now, you'd better get used to living in those back rooms. You've given up your right to your own street. After today, anyone out here is going to be your enemy.'

As we headed for the river I murmured, 'Would your superintendent entirely approve of putting the fear of God into a bunch of old ladies and village idiots?'

She shook her head angrily. 'They could have helped us if they'd wanted. They could at least have tried. Clio, I can walk into any street in any sink estate in London and find someone who'll stick his neck out to give help if it's needed. What makes these people think they can opt out? Got a note for teacher, have they, saying they're excused caring?'

I shrugged. 'You can't force people to behave decently. You can't legislate for people's consciences. Forget them. What could they have done anyway?'

'They could have tried,' she insisted. 'They could at least have tried.'

'You're right,' I decided. 'When this is over we'll come back and break some windows.'

She stopped then, staring at me. The anger had gone from her eyes; even the fear had found its own level. Mostly what I saw there was a kind of compassion. 'Come back? Clio, I thought you knew. What I said – that wasn't for effect. When this is over, we'll be dead.'

IV

Fourth Horseman

Twelve

The river was not one of the great waterways of the world. No one would ever design buildings to take advantage of the view, write poetry beside it or perform seductions on it. It was a drain of the kind we'd been falling into since we arrived here. It was a little wider, maybe the water moved in it a little less sluggishly, but essentially it was run-off for the marsh. Because the water was black you couldn't see the bottom, but it wouldn't be more than a few feet deep. For all her length, *Hereward* would draw less than a metre. Like all barges, she was designed to sail over a heavy dew.

She. I know it's nonsense, but if you spend any time with boats, particularly old boats, it's hard not to think of them as people. They develop ways of their own. Build two to the same specification and one will be a lady and one will be a bitch. One will scent out the wind when there's no wind there, and the other will lie like a brick while a gale howls about her. Also, they can express themselves. *Hereward* looked as surprised by all the activity round her as the tea lady at a Mecca ballroom who's nodded off in a comfortable chair and woken to find herself crowned Miss World.

I was surprised too. The plan had been to simulate activity to confuse the enemy. But instead of calling meaningless instructions to one another and giving the timbers an occasional thump with a shovel, Chase and Jimmy Ferris were energetically digging mud away from the bow. Saul was scuttling about the deck on his hands and knees, unimpeded by the disability that hampered him when he moved upright, laying out the remains of the rigging around John, who was apparently knitting but on closer inspection knotting, making a few long ropes out of the sound bits. Costigian was prowling the boat as deliberately as a caged animal about to rip its keeper's head off. Then he disappeared below.

Saul saw us coming and shouted, 'They're back,' a chord of excitement vibrating in his voice.

Costigian's head came out of the hold like a jack-in-the-box. 'We can make this work.'

I wanted to cry. 'You've got these people working their guts out trying to float a wreck?'

He shook his head. Rain and sweat had plastered his hair into his eyes. 'She's not a wreck. The hull's sound. It's sweated a bit, but that's better than the planks drying out and shrinking. OK, she wouldn't do the Fastnet race. But she only has to make ten miles.'

'How? With a diesel engine that you prepared earlier? Her rigging's minestone!'

'OK,' he agreed, undeterred. 'But how much of it's necessary? We have to make one passage, that's all. We need a forestay, a mainsheet and something to tie the yard up with. Maybe thirty metres all told. When John gets the best bits out of the cordage we'll have that much.'

'You'll have that much with knots every few feet,' I snapped. 'How are you going to make knots run through the blocks?'

'What blocks? This isn't the *Shamrock*, it's the Ark. One voyage, no trimmings. I'll tie the stay to the masthead and the forelead. The winch has gone, we'll have to manage without that. And the sail will be tied to the mast before it goes up. It'll be hard work but we're tough characters.' He grinned insanely. 'We're survivalists.'

He was right in one respect. A lot of the rigging on a sailing boat is to make her easier to handle. If we didn't care that once set *Hereward*'s rig would be as capable of fine-tuning as a steamroller, perhaps we could do it.

Except for one thing. He'd overlooked one thing and it was the death of his plan. Nothing else would work if we couldn't get the mast up. It was forty feet of timber: with the additional weight of the yard and the sail it would weigh as much as a tree. We had no winch, no crane, no sheerlegs. All we had was the strength of our arms and backs, and some of us hadn't even that. The great bleached spar that had lain on *Hereward*'s deck since Saul's grandfather retired would be lying there still when we were dead.

I said nastily, 'How are you going to get the mast up? Push it up with a broom?'

I waited for his face to fall. But instead he beckoned. 'Walk this way.'

Inside the hull smelled like a Chinese takeaway. The crumbling sweetness was left from her days as a carrier, a memory of grain and flour and animal feed. The sourness was the smell of slime on wet timber. And the salt was the same salt that was everywhere, on the shore and in the marsh and in the harbour and grained into the stones of the little village. Only here where the air went undisturbed for years at a time the tang had thickened to an almost palpable consistency, like curds thickening towards cheese.

Almost all a Norfolk wherry is hold. The mast is stepped in the bows, a Spartan cabin is spared in the stern for the needs of the crew, and everything else – ninety-five per cent of the boat – is cargo space. *Hereward* would once have carried twenty-five tons twenty miles a day for the cost of a man's wage and a boy's keep. I looked round, wondering what Costigian wanted me to see.

He nodded his head. 'What do you reckon?'

We had worked our way forward to the massive structure that marked the front of the hold. It was part of the basic construction of the boat, locked in with the laying of the keel and the heavy frames, its importance fundamental. 'That's the tabernacle. That's where the mast is stepped.'

'Right.' He led me back on deck. 'And that?'

Now I knew what he'd found that had made all the activity seem worthwhile: a ton and a half of lead bolted to the foot of the mast. The mast wasn't fixed in the tabernacle: it pivoted on a massive pin.

The bane of inland waterways in the days of sail was the bridges. A working boat had to be able to drop and raise its mast using only the strength of those on board, and a pivoting mast with a counterweight at the foot was how. When people like George Applegate of Potter Heigham were doing this daily they could drop the mast, shoot the bridge, raise the mast again and have the sail drawing before the boat lost way. Or so they said.

If it had worked for Applegate it should work for us. We hadn't his skill but there were more of us. The main thing was that, once that mast went up, we had to be ready to leave. A forty-foot mast with six hundred square feet of black sail on it would be visible from anywhere in the marsh.

'What do you think?' Costigian asked again, impatiently.

I thought it was possible: I didn't know if we could do it. The pin might have seized solid inside the mast. Or it might have corroded and under the weight of the gear would break and send the lead crashing through the bottom boards. So maybe it wasn't much of a chance; but it was more than we'd had half an hour ago.

When Marion said she expected us to die here I hadn't felt anything. Feeling is a privilege reserved for those with some kind of a future. For the damned it's a wasted effort. But now there was a chance for us. Maybe not a great one; maybe if we'd had any alternative except a man feeling his way across a black marsh we wouldn't have considered it. But it was a chance, and with it came hope, and with the hope came flooding, paralysing fear. I didn't know what to say. The magnitude of the task crushed the breath out of me. Finally I stammered, 'Maybe . . .'

His teeth made a wolfish gleam in the overcast. 'Maybe's what I made it too. Maybe'll do.' He turned and trotted the length of the boat, and by the time I'd got my breath back he was telling Marion what he planned, his head bent, the rain plastering the clothes to his broad frame.

Costigian sent Jimmy to drain oil from the sump of the van and he came back with a can of something like black treacle. It would do nothing to strengthen the pin but it might help free it. Everything depended on the mast going up when we needed it to.

He waited for the oil to penetrate, then Costigian took the crowbar to the stern where the topmast projected over the rail. Using a baulk of stout wood as a fulcrum, he jockeyed the claw of the jemmy under the spar and levered down on it.

Nothing happened. I was watching the pin, and none of the force he was applying reached it. I shook my head.

He shifted the fulcrum, adjusted the lever. When he threw all his weight on to it, the truck of the mast rose a hand-span off the counter. But a wooden mast isn't rigid; it's designed to have some play along its length. The timber was merely bending. I shook my head again. 'Nothing.'

Chase went to join him, lifting the heaviest plank he could find. He hadn't Costigian's bulk – for the first time since he'd left I wished we still had Hollis – but he was a strong man and he knew how to use his strength. He jammed the plank under the mast where it crossed the cabin top and put his shoulder under it. 'Try again.'

They tried again, both in concert, and again the truck lifted. With quick shuffling movements they worked their implements further under the mast and levered it higher. Their bodies bent in powerful arcs and the muscles bunched under their wet clothes. But there was no movement in the taber-nacle.

'It's no good, guys, the damn thing's seized solid.' Disappointment was like the lead weight in my voice.

Costigian's head swung round like an angry bear's. He was ready to break his body rather than be beaten by that mast, but there was nothing more he could do. He had swung his whole weight on the crowbar and it hadn't been enough. Now he took the plank wedged between the mast and the cabin top and gave Chase the crowbar.

'What difference will *that* make?' demanded Marion, plain-tive with despair.

But there was a difference. Pulling down on the jemmy, the amount of force the big man could exert was limited by his own weight – if he pulled harder than that, he left the deck. Levering up, the only limiting factor was his strength. If he could lift more than his own weight, this was a way to tap into that potential. He bent low and got his shoulder under the beam. Then, with a quick grin at me, he shifted it to his undamaged side. He looked at Chase. 'Ready?'

'When you are.'

Without another word the big Canadian began to straighten.

111

Timber groaned like a man in pain. The truck of the mast lifted higher than it had gone before. Chase jammed the block further under his crowbar: soon after that he was able to discard the bar and get his shoulder under the mast.

The muscles of both men were huge with effort. Tendons stood out on their necks like cables. Their faces were slab-like with tension, glowing with sweat, their expressions distant, all their energy tuned to the struggle.

The mast made a louder protest. Watching the pin, I saw oil bubble out round it as if some fraction of all that effort had finally worked its way to the tabernacle. 'Yes!' I shouted. 'Something's happening . . .'

Costigian had himself almost straightened out. All up his arms and across his shoulders the muscles stood proud. His teeth were clenched and his eyes stared whitely. He groaned like the cracking timber.

By my elbow Marion whispered, 'He's going to kill himself.' Her voice was a cocktail of the bull-fight emotions: admiration and horror and grief and fear and wonder.

She was right. The human body isn't designed to take that kind of stress. If the immovable object didn't yield soon, the irresistible force would have to. If he wouldn't accept defeat, if he kept trying beyond the bounds of what was physically possible, something cataclysmic would happen, in his heart or in his head.

'Clio,' gritted Marion. 'Stop him.'

I opened my mouth to shout a warning – to tell him to stop now, for God's sake stop before his heart burst – and then I shut it again. What did it matter if he killed himself? We were all dead if he didn't succeed. I whispered instead, 'A little more – only a little more . . .' and caught Marion's appalled glance on my cheek like a blow.

More bubbles in the oil round the pin. I touched the mast with my fingertips and felt it alive. Startled, I looked along the spar and met the agony in Costigian's face.

Before there was time to say or do anything more there was a great rending crack as the years of rust and inertia broke. The truck of the mast leapt two metres into the air and only came down when we grabbed the canvas of the sail.

The heavy plank flew out of Costigian's hands and fell on the boards, and the big man sank on his knees as if the crack had been every bone in his body breaking.

Thirteen

He'd re-opened the wound on his arm. While I dressed it we clustered on the deck, planning.

'Are you two agreed?' asked Marion. 'This is going to work? That was the last obstacle?'

Costigian was so tired I shrugged for both of us. 'So far as we can tell. If we can raise the mast we can sail her. Christ!' I looked aft in sudden alarm. 'Is there a rudder?' Propulsion was of limited value if we couldn't steer.

'Yes,' said Saul. There was no doubt in his voice so I didn't go and check. In the depths of his beard there was a secret smile as his dream took shape.

I smiled back, but I was troubled. These people had trusted me to judge if *Hereward* could take us out of here. They'd trusted me with their lives. And I'd glanced her up and down and decided she was crow-bait. But for Costigian we'd have thrown away our last hope of leaving here before Growth Industries came for us.

Marion was peering at me anxiously. I shook off the spectre of blame. Yes, I was wrong; and yes, it could have cost us all our lives; but it hadn't, and we all have to live with our mistakes – if we're lucky. 'Sorry. Yes. She won't sail well, but she'll sail.'

'How long to get her ready?'

That wasn't really the point. If we left as soon as we'd dug her out, the tide would be against us. In her day the Norfolk wherry had a good name for pointing into a headwind – what George Applegate called a 'dead muzzler'. But that was with her hull clean and her rigging tuned. *Hereward* would be tied together with string and she wasn't going to win any luffing matches.

I did some quick calculations. 'It'll be high water about seven this evening. That's the time to go, when we've six hours of ebb and the whole night ahead of us.'

John said, 'What if they come before that?'

If they came for us, we had two choices: to go with them or to fight; to die like bulls or like sheep. 'Then they'll probably kill us. I'm sorry, John. I'm sorry I can't give you a guarantee. I think we have a chance this way. I think waiting for the tide will give us a better chance than going sooner. I could be wrong. It's my best guess.'

I was kneeling on the deck with my hands on my thighs. John leaned over, his face grey with sickness, and laid his palm over one of them. 'Take no notice of me, I'm just trying to make a contribution.'

Costigian had enough breath to talk now. 'Then get knotting. We're going to need all the rope we can get.'

I found Chase once more digging at the bow. 'You are coming with us, aren't you?'

He shook his head. 'Better to keep another option open. This might not work. If the *Keith and Mary* comes back, you won't be able to hide from her even in the dark. But as long as they don't get all of us, they won't dare . . .' He balked at saying it. 'If I'm on the loose, they have to assume I could get through. And if they pick me up, I'll be safe as long as you're at large. We need to split our resources.'

I looked to Marion for support, but she agreed with him. 'I couldn't tackle that marsh alone. But if you think you can, then yes – I think that would be best.'

Perhaps it comes down to what you're used to. Chase was right, but my instincts said we'd be safe once *Hereward* was at sea. I hated to think of him slogging it out alone in that black swamp, surrounded by enemies, every step he took liable to tumble him into liquid mud that would hold him and drown him slowly. But perhaps he felt the same way about the wherry. I dropped my gaze, and he smiled and picked up his spade and went on digging.

Now we were doing this for real it was important that GI believed in the hopelessness of the task. If we seemed to be making progress, they'd stop us. So at intervals we took turns to throw down our shovels in disgust, stump away and sulk. Sometimes we had loud arguments about the pointlessness of the enterprise.

Twice Saul left us for a while, his twisted body swinging between his crutches up the path to the village, to check on his mother and George. The second time he came back at speed and lurched over to where I was working, and this boy who wouldn't bend before the humiliations every day visited on him had tears on his cheeks. 'It's my ma. Will you come?'

I imagined she was ill, but that wasn't it. I found her dressed, sitting on the edge of her bed, squeezing into shoes that were too small for her swollen feet. Beside her was a suitcase and she had a hat on. 'I'm going to visit Mrs Boston for a few days.'

I nodded, feeling my way. 'Where does she live?'

Mrs Penny beamed. 'Two doors along.'

We sent Saul to make some sandwiches for the voyage, and we talked. She said, 'I want him to go with you. He won't leave me here alone, so I'm going to Mrs Boston.'

I bit my lip. 'Coming with us could be dangerous, Mrs Penny.'

She was an intelligent woman. She knew what I was saying. Perhaps she'd heard Marion's soliloquy in the street. 'I know that. But what he's done already is dangerous. He helped you against them, and they won't forget that. Everybody here keeps out of their way, but not my Saul. It's a kind of pride with him. You know why. They've put up with it because of how he is, because till now he couldn't be any more than a nuisance; but they won't put up with this. I want him out. The only way is with you. I know it's dangerous. I think, for Saul, staying would be more dangerous.'

Perhaps she was right. If they meant to kill us they had to be sure no one would talk. Those who'd helped by taking away the boats we could have used to leave or by turning their backs on murder were safe. But Saul had no reason to fear the police, and every reason to hate GI, and no one at the plant would sleep easily with him on the loose. If they killed us, they'd kill him too.

I shrugged helplessly. 'Of course we'll take him if it's

what you want. I just don't want to mislead you. This is a last resort. We're only trying it because we can't stay here.'

'Listen, dear,' she said briskly, 'I can't know what's for the best any more than you can. Maybe I'm wrong, but I think he'll be better with you. I don't regret what Saul's done. It was time someone stood up to them. But if he stays here because of me, I'll be sorry for that. I'm going to Mrs Boston, and I want Saul to come with you, and that's all I have to say.'

We helped her round to Mrs Boston's house. Saul wouldn't wait for the door to be answered: he lurched away and waited at the corner, staring up into the rain, his head tipped back against the wall.

Before I joined him I had one last question that I couldn't have asked with him there. 'Mrs Penny, Saul thinks his disability has something to do with the plant. Do you?'

She looked at me as if I'd asked what day of the week it was. 'Why, bless you, dear, of course it has. I don't know that it was anybody's fault – maybe it was just one of those things – but that's where it came from for sure.'

'Your doctor told you that?'

She laughed out loud. 'Don't be daft! Doctors never tell you anything like that. If they can't blame you for what's happened, they blame God. God can't sue them, see? No, the doctors said it was just bad luck. They thought at first maybe I'd done too much – I was walking from here to the plant and back all the time I was pregnant, but what's a few miles' walking to a healthy girl? These days they tell you to walk, don't they?'

I nodded.

'I never listened much to what they said anyway. None of my family had any trouble with babies. Damn things crawled out of the woodwork any time you weren't watching. But my sister died barren, and my only child was born crooked, and there's hardly been a baby born on The Island since the plant opened. Something in the air, I guess. Maybe they didn't know; or maybe they decided it was the price we had to pay for an affluent society.' She smiled, ruefully but without bitterness.

Then Mrs Boston came and took her inside, and closed the door quietly in my face.

Back at *Hereward* I told Marion, 'Saul's coming with us.' Just that, no elaboration. She nodded. No one else said anything; we kept digging and, at intervals, squabbling.

When we had done all we could, we headed back to The Wake, ostensibly having given up our futile labour, in fact to raid the pub for food, blankets, buckets for bailing, and anything else we could use in our dash for freedom. But John stayed where he was, sitting on the gunwale, and when I called him he looked round with a sick smile and said, 'I don't think I can make it that far.'

I hadn't realized how wretched he was feeling. All the time there had been work to do he'd kept working, and if it cost him blood he kept it to himself. Now the work was finished and he'd allowed himself to stop, illness swept over him like a fog. His eyes weren't focusing, his skin was ghostly and he was too dizzy to stand.

I took him below, got him out of the wettest of his things, bundled him up in the driest of everyone else's and made a bed for him in a corner of the hold. It was all I could do for him. He was sick and going to get sicker, and all I could do was try to keep him warm and stop him wandering off.

I found Costigian at my shoulder. 'Is that . . . ?'

'Yes.' It was what killed Nick. But it didn't have to kill John. We knew what to expect; we could watch him, keep him safe – as safe as any of us, anyway. I changed the subject. 'Can I ask you something?'

'Sure.'

'You and Marion. Is it only coincidence that you're here together?'

He snorted with amusement. 'You think we're so fond of one another we take joint holidays?'

'I hoped it might be – I don't know – an undercover operation, an investigation of some kind. But I suppose if it had been, we'd have been rescued by now.'

He nodded apologetically. He'd thought it was mere inquisitiveness. But in our present situation no one's business was his own. Anything that affected any of us affected us all. 'Sorry, no. It was pretty much a coincidence. There was an item on the survival school in the *Police Review*: that's where

I got the idea. I guess Fletcher saw the same thing.'

'Tell me about it,' I said wearily. I'd seen the same article in my husband Harry's copy. It was a wonder the group wasn't composed entirely of police officers, all pretending to be something else. 'But you do know one another.'

He nodded. 'I was on a year's secondment over here. With the Met.' He grinned, without much mirth. 'Listen to me: I sound like a bona fide English bobby.'

'Not really,' I said. 'So you and Marion were working together?'

'Only once. It was a big operation, they called in spare hands from all over the city.'

'What happened?'

What happened was that Special Branch had been watching a house near King's Cross for three weeks. It was owned by a Saudi national who seemed to have a lot of lodgers and even more visitors, and they came and went mostly by night and carried large holdalls a lot. There was no clear evidence that it was a terrorist cell at work. None of the usual suspects had been seen at the house. Nevertheless, it was only prudent to wonder if a large group of Saudis, Pakistanis and Jordanians, all men, mostly under thirty, unnecessarily discreet about their comings and goings, might have something in mind besides improving their English.

'After three weeks,' said Costigian, 'opinion was divided. Half the team thought their behaviour was suspicious enough to justify a dawn raid. The other half reckoned that all the men were guilty of was being persistently Arab in a built-up area.'

'Which side did you take?' I asked quietly.

'I thought it was a case of buck fever. I doubted anyone would have thought they were terrorists if they'd been white.'

'If the same group had gathered in Toronto, you wouldn't have done anything about them?'

'I wouldn't.' He shrugged. 'My superiors might have. It's easy to give people the benefit of the doubt when you aren't the one who's going to have to – literally – pick up the pieces. Anyway, the decision was taken to search the house.'

The possibility of explosives had been at the front of everyone's mind. A specialist group had been put together including technical and firearms officers. Marion and Costigian had been roped in under the latter category.

My eyebrows rocketed. 'Marion totes a gun?'

'When she has to. Her rating was as good as anyone's there. Well, nearly.'

I squinted at him. 'There was someone better qualified?'

'I've had more practice,' he said briefly. 'Anyway, we were given different points of entry. She and I were in the team that went up the back steps.'

And on a signal – more reliable than synchronizing watches – big guys with rams had knocked in the front and back doors, and maybe a window as well, and twenty armed police officers had poured into the house. There had been shouting, in different languages, and other signs of panic as the young men woke to find themselves being overrun by strangers in body armour.

'There was a lot of running about. We needed to pin them down quickly so no one could detonate a device. Me and Marion and another guy followed one kid up the back stairs and cornered him in the washroom.'

A kid? So this was when . . . ?

'He was terrified. Shit-scared. There were no explosives in there and he'd no means of detonating them if there had been. But there was a big window. He threw it open and climbed out. We were four floors up: he was going to fall and be killed. And I thought the only thing he'd done wrong was to want to study in a city that was half-expecting a terrorist attack. I dived at his feet as they disappeared over the sill.'

He was a bigger man than the boy halfway through the window and he'd managed to hold him and pull him back. Marion was shouting at him to be careful but Costigian had ignored her. So had their colleague, who'd holstered his weapon and come to help. Within a few seconds they'd had the boy, yelling and shaking hysterically, down on the bathroom floor and Costigian had turned to shut the window.

'He pulled the gun out of my holster,' he said quietly. 'He shoved it under my vest and pulled the trigger. Then he shot the other guy in the face.'

I was making an effort to control my breathing. 'And Marion?'

'Marion took him out.'

She'd killed someone. She'd had to shoot dead an eighteen-year-old boy. 'And she blamed you.'

'Yeah. I guess she was right. If I'd followed procedure the kid would have fallen to his death. I broke it, and a colleague died as well. It was a bad call. Not stupid, not reckless – the inquiry decided it had been reasonable in all the circumstances – but it was wrong. I should have let him fall.'

I vented an unsteady sigh. 'And were they terrorists?'

'Yes,' he nodded. 'I was wrong about that too.'

Most people are never called upon to make life-and-death decisions. Of those that are, the hardest – the ones that lead to recurring nightmares – are the ones that you have to take on the basis not of what has happened but of what might happen. Some people freeze and never make the call, and that can be disastrous too. Others take their best guess and keep their fingers crossed. If it works out badly, as it had for Costigian, all you can do is set it against some other time when the runes fell more propitiously.

I said, 'Life's a bitch,' and he nodded.

Soon after that the rest of them came back from The Wake with George and all the supplies they could carry without it showing.

Eight hours had passed since the battle lines were drawn. All afternoon we'd been expecting a new assault. But GI was giving us time to become bored and embarrassed, and sidle back to the plant to talk. The more time that passed with nothing to show for it, the readier we would be to surrender our limited freedom for another shot at those showers and the hope that we might have misunderstood.

But at some point, when we didn't come trooping disconsolately up the road, they would come for us. If we had seemed to be achieving anything, they'd have been here before now; anyway they would come before night. All we were waiting for was the tide.

Chase was staying at The Wake until after we sailed. When

they saw *Hereward* heading out, GI would assume we were all on board. With luck, every spare hand would be committed to intercepting us and a man moving carefully would not be seen as dusk swallowed the marsh.

At twenty to seven, still with no sign of movement on the causeway, the river was full, *Hereward* unmistakably afloat. A big boat doesn't bob around like a dinghy but the deck under our feet was alive, quite different from when she'd been held in the mud. The rudder was lying in the stern, waiting to be shipped, and we had the big quant ready to pole her out into the river.

Questions filled my mind. Would the mast go up, taking the heavy sail with it? Would the forestay we'd cobbled together hold? Would the black sail draw or would it split along every seam? And if it drew, could we handle it without all the tackle designed to reduce the task to a human scale?

The wind was full of squalls and running straight down The Wash like a ferret down a trouser-leg. A nice broad reach on a Force 3 westerly would have carried us to safety on a garage door with a pair of bloomers for a sail, but this clearly wasn't meant to be easy. We were committed, however, so at quarter to seven we poled *Hereward* out of her mud-berth and into the river.

We wanted to get to sea as quickly as possible, before GI could react. So for a few minutes longer we left the mast untouched. Instead Costigian applied himself to the quant. Three and a half metres long – a mere stripling compared with George Applegate's twenty-footer – it was essentially a stick with a steel fork at one end and a shoulder-rest at the other. With the fork thrust into the river bed and the bott lodged in his shoulder, the wherryman walked from the bow to the stern, by which time the boat had travelled fifty feet. Then he did it again, and again. Men who spent half their working lives quanting developed the sort of musculature you normally only see on a Belgian Blue bull. Nobody jogged *their* elbows in riverside pubs.

Costigian had the build for it. He didn't have the shoulder for it, but you wouldn't have known from watching him. He kept walking and poling, walking and poling until the curve of the river took us around the low prominence that was The Island and we saw the silver line of The Wash ahead.

Safety beckoned, but we weren't safe yet. The river was only narrow: with a minimum of time and initiative GI could run a boom across to stop us. Shotguns would be pretty effective at this range too. The dark flint houses, low to the street, perched high over the river and we couldn't see who was watching; but we felt eyes on us all the way. The villagers of Graveleigh, who experienced such problems with their hearing, apparently had no trouble with their sight.

Then the houses were past and the stone wall of the harbour loomed. There was no movement that I could see, but that didn't mean we hadn't been spotted. Every ATV on the marsh was probably racing down here right now.

When we passed the harbour wall, at last we were out of range of any assault from the land. The marsh flattened darkly behind us, The Wash shone silver ahead and the mud dropped away under our keel. When the water was too deep for the quant Costigian handed it to me, fork uppermost. 'Let's get the mast up. Once it starts to lift, push it up with that.' He gave Marion and Jimmy the job of hauling on the forestay, arming himself with the heavy plank he'd used to good effect earlier.

None of which would matter a damn if the lead at its foot wasn't enough to lift the mast, the yard and the heavy canvas sail. We thought it would: it was designed for the job. But there was only one way to find out.

George Applegate would have been proud of us. I dare say he did it better, but it all came together smoother than I'd dared hope. As Costigian levered the mast up, the lead swung down and momentum kept the whole thing in motion until the weight of the yard made it falter. But by then I was able to get the quant under the mast: with Costigian and me both pushing and Marion and Jimmy swinging on the forestay the mast completed its arc against the sky. When the lead seated in the bottom of the tabernacle, the whole boat shook.

By now the great faded sail, daylight showing through in places, was flapping above us, loose-footed, drumming and cracking in the wind. If you've never heard it, you can't imagine the noise of setting sail in a strong breeze. You can't believe it isn't doing incalculable harm. And of course, left to flap it would. When great spreads of canvas moved the world's trade across the world's seas, it wasn't the sails that were sheeted hard and stretched by fifty-knot winds that split, it was the one that was allowed to flog.

That was the danger now: that in the time it took us to secure our knotty lines the sail would have flogged to streamers. When they'd finished making fast, the others came aft and we all stared upwards. Then we exchanged anxious *What do you think?* looks, and shrugged and nodded. It wasn't America's Cup class rigging, but it might do.

It was time to see whether *Hereward* would sail. If she wouldn't, all our efforts had been wasted, and even that was the least of our worries. Above the thunder of the sail Costigian shouted, 'Saul – take her away!'

For a few agonizing seconds nothing happened. Saul had the rudder hard over, but without headway she wasn't answering. He sawed at the tiller with all the power of his massive shoulders; and a degree at a time the bow came off the wind and the sail stopped flogging and assumed a tentative roundness.

Then with another crack it filled. The wherry heeled under the pressure. I watched the forestay with my heart in my mouth – if it parted we were lost. But it held. As the boat began to move forward she stood up again; and the mast was holding, and the sail was holding, and the rudder was guiding her across the angle of the waves, and Graveleigh was slipping away behind us.

We'd done it. We'd taken a derelict that was fit only for firewood and cobbled together the means for her to make one more passage; and we'd sailed her out of the corner we'd been backed into, and if our luck held the rain would bring an early dusk, under cover of which we could go on sailing until we were safe.

I looked back. That shape on the harbour wall shrinking behind us was two men beside an ATV, silhouetted against the westering day. One of them raised a hand in the air. He might have been waving, but somehow I doubted it.

Fourteen

For ten minutes we enjoyed the glorious sense of escape, and the cold wind blustering in the face, the rain pouring off the sail, the pitching, rolling motion of the sea.

At first I was afraid *Hereward* might knock down. Where *Grainne* was built for the turbulent Atlantic, *Hereward* was essentially a river boat. She hadn't the depth of hull that allowed the hooker to dig into the seas and let the wind blow over her. But Saul was a sensitive helmsman and he knew her tolerances and how to stay the right side of them. The state of the sail might have helped: as much wind blew through it as pressed on it.

There was a certain amount of water coming aboard. The low stem dug into the wave tops and sent silver rivers running down the decks. I hoped that most of it was clearing over the lee gunwale, but after ten minutes I went below to check and found John's makeshift bunk awash.

Some of it was foaming over the bows, but some of it was coming through the boards. The leverage exerted by the sail had opened cracks in her that years in the mud had not discovered. And we were still a long way from any shore we wanted to land on.

Saul gave me the helm and organized a bailing relay. His powerful arms lifted the full buckets as if on some primitive machine and slung them to Marion on deck, who emptied them and threw them back. Costigian fed buckets to Jimmy in the same way.

George said to me, apologetically, 'I can't do that, but I can steer if you want to help Marion.'

With all of us at it we could keep the water level from rising, but we would be bailing for as long as we were at sea.

Night shaded in imperceptibly from the east. First the sky paled, then a semicircle of dusk closed down half the horizon; finally the light went to just a few oyster-coloured streaks that travelled down the sky and sank in the marsh.

The night was a friend to us. We could not be seen, nor could our progress be predicted or our way barred. Every tack out into The Wash increased the area of watery waste we could get lost in. They couldn't guess if we'd head east for the Norfolk coast or north towards Lincolnshire. I thought we were safe until dawn, and I hoped that dawn would find me sobbing on the broad blue shoulder of the sergeant of a small seaside police station.

All the same, the night brought its own problems. The thick wrack of cloud swallowed the stars so we couldn't be sure where we were. And there's a lot of shallow water round the margins of The Wash. Shallow water is water enough for a boat drawing two and a half feet, but even a wherry can't sail up a beach. We could watch for breakers and listen for the rush of shingle, but if we came down on mud, the first we would know would be the shuddering deceleration as the bow bit into the bottom.

While those who could bailed and I steered, George took himself into the forepeak with a spanner on three metres of rope. If he found bottom, it was time to put about. Hunched round the misery of his broken collarbone, he sat in the rain and the spray, heaving the makeshift lead one-handedly, sounding the waves as we beat first one way across The Wash, then the other.

I needed to check on John. Saul took the helm while I went below.

Every time I looked at him he was worse, and out here there was nothing I could do for him. I couldn't keep him dry, I couldn't make him warm, I couldn't make him well. He'd been violently sick and now he'd gone terribly quiet. I was afraid he was lapsing into a coma.

Marion had followed me below. 'How's he doing?' She sounded utterly exhausted.

'Not great.' It was world-class understatement, but there was no point sharing my fears. If I couldn't help him, no one else could. I was going to lose another one.

But she read my mind and her arm hugged my shoulder. 'Nick didn't die of this. He died because we couldn't keep him from wandering off into the marsh. John's going to make it.' From somewhere she dredged up the sound of conviction.

Three hours ago, waiting while the long afternoon dragged away, I had thought that when we were at sea our problems would be over. Now it seemed the celebrations would have to wait.

I wanted to stay with him, but either Saul or I had to be at the helm and he was needed to bail. I left Marion below and went to relieve him. He was moving forward crabwise along the deck when the topping-lift broke.

It wasn't a topping-lift except in name. It was a bit of rope with which we'd tied the yard to the mast. We hadn't had enough to rig it properly, had merely cobbled together something to hold the peak of the sail up. And it had held – right up to the moment when it didn't.

That yard was ten metres long, and if it was of lighter timber than the mast it was still too damn heavy to be dropping on people's heads. It scythed down in a great arc and the tip plunged into the sea, throwing up a gout of spray that slashed across the boat. There wasn't even time to shout a warning.

Apart from George on the foredeck and me in the stern, everyone on board was midships when it fell. The collapsing sail buried them all and the yard crushed the coaming to matchwood.

I abandoned the tiller – with no sail *Hereward* had no need of a helmsman – and scrabbled frantically at the billows of canvas. I had no idea what I'd find beneath – people or carnage.

I found Costigian, and he wasn't digging his way out but digging his way in. He was unhurt: the spar had crashed by centimetres from his knee without touching him. Together we clawed at the wet canvas, amorphous as whale skin, damning the dark.

Then we heard voices, querulous with shock, and someone

found the torch and we could see what had happened. We'd been lucky. No one had suffered more than a buffeting from the sail. We had a hold full of startled people and wet canvas, and a nasty dent in the gunwale, but the crucial thing was that we'd lost our sail and with it all hope of reaching a friendly harbour before dawn. As sailing boats go, *Hereward* was now a piece of driftwood. We would slosh around on top of the tide until someone picked us up. Since the only ones looking for us were Growth Industries, rescue seemed a forlorn hope.

'There must be *something* we can do,' insisted Marion angrily.

And actually there was. We could make our crappy great sail into an even crappier small one, and if we no longer had much say in where we went, at least we would be going somewhere. We couldn't sail out of The Wash to freedom, but perhaps we could reach shore and disappear into the salt-ings and maybe even find help before GI knew where to look for us. What we couldn't do was sail upwind. We had to turn back.

When we had lashed the spar to the mast, and pulled the much-reduced triangle of canvas into some semblance of a sail, we let *Hereward*'s head come round until we were under way again. I told my companions we were aiming for Lincolnshire near the Witham estuary. But I knew that we were just as likely to sail right back into Graveleigh.

For a couple of hours we stumbled on through the chop produced by an onshore wind over an ebb tide. By now it was the very early morning, cold and pitch-black, and Marion and the men were bailing and I was steering, and all of us were mentally and physically exhausted, working on autopilot.

George had stopped sounding. If I found a shore now I was going to sail clean up it. But he'd settled with his back against the tabernacle, and he was still there when some-thing the size of a super-tanker came at him out of the black. He yelled and rolled away from it.

By now we were wide awake, trying desperately to make sense of what he'd seen. There was still no light to help, only a baleful red eye above our starboard bow. Picking out the shape was a matter of juggling black and blacker, but there was no doubting the size of the thing. If it hit us there wouldn't be enough left of *Hereward* for seven of us to cling to.

I pushed the tiller away from me, trying to pass the bigger vessel upwind. But *Hereward* couldn't point any more. I felt the way going off her, felt her dropping back on to a collision course, knew that with no speed and no steering there was nothing more I could do. I stared open-mouthed at the black bulk and waited for the splintering impact.

Hereward butted her nose gently against the steel jetty of the Growth Industries terminal. We tied her up there and, when our racing hearts permitted, considered what to do next.

We had one thing in our favour: GI didn't know we were there. The security hut was at the landward end of the jetty, the soft jar of our collision shouldn't have reached the guard through half a mile of steelwork. But when the sun came up he'd see us.

I thought we had two choices: to stay where we were, or to work the wherry round the jetty and let her carry us as far as she could along the shore before beaching. We might make another mile that way. But we'd still be cut off from help by the marsh, and we'd still be seen as soon as the sun rose.

Costigian had another idea. 'We stay on the jetty, but we make it look like we were on the boat when she went down. We push her off and let the wind take her. With no one bailing she'll founder in ten minutes – especially if we knock some more holes in her. When the sun comes up, there'll be nothing to see but a bit of floating wreckage and maybe the top of the mast sticking out of the sea.'

It was bold, and unexpected, and I liked it. Their own property was the last place they'd look for us. We could stay at the terminal, keeping out of sight, for days if we had to. There was rain enough to keep an army from thirst, and fasting wouldn't kill us. By then, surely to God someone would have missed us? Better yet, maybe Chase had got through the marsh and was even now returning with help.

All we had to do was stay out of sight until someone turned up in a police car rather than an ATV.

Saul was horrified. 'You're not punching holes in my boat!'

I tried to reason with him. 'All our lives may depend on it . . .'

'I don't care! She's my boat. She was my grandfather's boat. She did her level best for you and I'm not having you punch holes in her because it wasn't good enough.'

We could have overpowered him and gone ahead. But we had enemies enough without making another one.

'Tell you what,' he said then, and his tone – we still couldn't see one another – was calmer. 'Help me get her round the jetty and shove us off. I'll stay with her. I won't sink her, but I'll sail her as far up the coast as I can. When she takes the ground, I'll hide in the marsh. If they find me, I'll tell them the rest of you escaped, only I couldn't keep up. And if they don't find me they'll assume we all escaped. Won't that do?' His voice was a plea.

There was a pause. Then Marion said, 'Yes,' and it was decided. Maybe it wasn't as good a plan as Costigian's. Maybe it kept GI searching for us after they might have given up. But Saul Penny had gone out on a limb for us, and nobody begrudged him the chance to save his boat.

It took us time to transfer to the jetty. Now the tide was low the terminal towered over us: it was a long climb up a steel ladder. George needed help. We hauled John up on a rope.

The doors of the terminal building were all locked. Costigian forced one at the seaward end. We found an office and made ourselves at home there.

Costigian went back to help Saul work *Hereward* round the jetty. They used the quant to push her along the steel construct until she cleared it. By then the reduced canvas was tugging, so Costigian climbed back on to the jetty and Saul sailed away.

Our safety depended on silence so we didn't wish him luck. We waved in the dark, and guessed that he was waving too.

Fifteen

We had started off a company of nine – ten if you counted Saul. Now Nick was dead, Terry Hollis had changed sides, Tom Chase was alone in the marsh and Saul had sailed away into the darkness, and we were six. When John died, we would be five.

Because he was going to die. Maybe a hospital could have saved him but I couldn't: not here on the tip of a steel finger pointing half a mile out to sea, with no equipment, no facilities, no lab to tell me what was wrong with him, no drugs to cure it. He was so close to death that we shouldn't really have moved him off the boat. To be honest, we did it not in his interests but in Saul's.

I was trained as a doctor: when I could do nothing more for a patient, I was meant to be inured to the trauma of death. Well, it doesn't quite work like that – you never quite shake off the sense of shock, of failure, of feeling that you could somehow have done better – but at least I wasn't going to feel anything I hadn't felt before. Saul Penny wasn't much more than a boy. I wouldn't wave him off into the dark knowing that when dawn came his only companion would be a corpse.

There wasn't much more I could do for George either. He wasn't in any danger but there was a lot of pain in spite of Mrs Penny's pills. He didn't complain, but the catch in his breathing plucked at my gut like another failure.

We mapped out the office by touch, without turning on the light. If we betrayed our presence here, we'd have nowhere to retreat to. When everyone had found somewhere to sprawl, at ease if not in comfort, Marion spelled out the ground rules. No lights, no noise and no one outside after daybreak. If we were still here at nightfall, we could get any exercise we needed then.

Soon after that the huddled shapes of my companions began to emerge from the blackness as the windows at each end of the long narrow office paled towards grey. The sun wasn't up yet but the eastern sky was receiving its first harbinger rays. Costigian got up laboriously, as if his body was thirty per cent heavier than usual, and looked out westward. 'I wonder if we can see the boat.' But the faded black canvas remained invisible against the dark sea. He said, 'I'm going to have a look round before it gets too light. Where's the torch?'

I started to pass it to him, but Marion interrupted sharply. 'I don't want any lights . . .'

'Don't worry, I won't let it be seen. But I want to know exactly what there is out here, and once it's light I won't be able to go and look.' He took the torch and Marion raised no further objection.

A few minutes later I looked out of the same window and this time *Hereward* was just visible, a deep shadow where the sea was brightening from black to pewter. She'd got further than I'd expected and was still half a mile offshore. She might make the Witham yet. I had mixed feelings about that. It improved Saul's chances of finding help; but the longer he was at sea, the longer GI had to spot him and stop him. I'd seen him because I'd known where to look. Half an hour from now anyone glancing out to sea would have to be blind to miss him.

Costigian came back. He hadn't been long because there wasn't much to see. 'The rest of the building's one big shed. There's a row of vats in there, some pipes and a bank of instruments. That's about all. There's only us here, but the security hut's manned – there's a light on.'

Marion said quickly, 'They didn't see you?'

He shook his head. 'No.'

Still my heart was racing. Perhaps the terminal was always guarded, but today that guard was looking for us. He hadn't seen us because the jetty was half a mile long, it was dark, *Hereward* was a wherry not a twin-engined powerboat, and all his instincts told him that any threat to the terminal would come from the land. But he was close enough to see us if we gave him anything to see, hear us if we made much noise, and maybe find us anyway if his job description involved coming out here at intervals to check the terminal.

Costigian was watching *Hereward*. 'I thought the old cow would have sunk by now.' Then in a different tone of voice: 'Hey . . .'

As the day poured slow as molten silver down The Wash another shadow resolved itself into a boat. It was a few miles away when we first saw it, heading for the Norfolk coast. But as we watched, it altered course, swinging round in a wide arc, turning first in our direction, then in Saul's.

'Have they seen him?'

I couldn't tell. *Hereward* was only a low dark sail on a dark hull and hardly enough metal aboard to register on radar. The boat might have been following a search grid. Out there was where GI would hope to find us if we hadn't made landfall by now. Or maybe it was only her fish-finder she was following. Growth Industries couldn't have suborned every fishing vessel on the east coast. A crew from Lowestoft might well investigate if they spotted the improbable *Hereward*.

And if they picked up Saul, they'd come here next and the thing would be over. Maybe even John . . . ? I didn't know if there was still time to save him, but I couldn't keep my heart from leaping to the sharp spurs of hope.

A modern trawler covers a couple of miles in under ten minutes. But it felt longer. All the time the morning was brightening – the sky was still leaden with rain clouds so there was no one glorious moment when the sun rose – and the trawler was drawing closer, and we were crowded together at the window trying to pick out some distinguishing feature. But all I could remember of the *Keith and Mary* was the name, and the trawler was still over a mile away when she passed us.

But I thought, Saul will know. If it's the *Keith and Mary*, he'll turn away, try to make the beach. If it's any of the dozens of other trawlers that might stray into The Wash, he'll turn to meet her. But then I thought, Maybe he can't. Jury-rigged as she was, *Hereward* wouldn't give him much manoeuvrability. With the devil on his tail he might have to hold his course.

The minutes ticked by, the seconds stretching and crawling. The trawler seemed to move in slow motion and *Hereward*, because she was stern-on to us, seemed not to move at all. Her hull disappeared intermittently in the troughs of the sea, her forty-foot mast stunted by the loss of her great sail. The skimpy surviving triangle was an apologetic bulge at the bottom.

The trawler narrowed the gap between them steadily. She was much bulkier than *Hereward*, built for a tough trade in some of the roughest waters in the world. Her bow, strong and sharp to cut into the hearts of black seas, loomed over the wherry as they closed. Some trick of perspective made it look as if she would cut *Hereward* clean in half.

She never faltered. All the power of the big diesels was driving her when the high sharp bow cut into *Hereward*'s flank. From more than a mile away we saw how the mast rocked wildly and the bastard sail bellied and flapped, and how the stern reared up out of the sea as her back was broken.

The trawler seemed hardly to notice the impact. She trod the wreckage down and motored through the space that a moment before had been occupied by the Norfolk wherry *Hereward* and the young man Saul Penny; and after the mast went, dragged to the bottom by a ton and a half of lead, nothing of the murdered boat remained.

People handle shock in different ways. I don't know if any of them are better or worse than any others.

I heard sobbing. Jimmy had his teeth set in his clenched hand and he was shaking and sobbing uncontrollably, tears chasing one another down his cheeks. A week ago this young man had been torn between petty crime and football hooliganism as a career. Now he'd had one friend die and seen another murdered, and the pain of that had rocked him to his foundations.

The low dull monotone of swearing, all the filthiest words you ever heard strung together without sense or pattern, just a thick slow torrent of obscenity welling up from some abyss of the human spirit, was George – affable, kindly George, whose own hurts had drawn hardly a murmur out of him. Now he cursed with vile fluency in bitterness, frustration and grief.

Marion seemed kicked back to some training exercise she'd once taken part in. The red hair was startling against the white skin, her lips were tight and bloodless, and she was repeating formulae with the terse desperation of someone who didn't dare let herself think. 'Now, I shall want statements from all of you.' Her voice had the peculiar glassy flatness of an Icelandic lake before the geyser erupts. 'So I don't want you discussing it first. You all know what you saw. I'll get some paper and pencils ...' She rummaged busily through the drawers and filing cabinets.

I demonstrated a piece of typical medical displacement activity: I took a pulse. It was John's, but any pulse would have done. If there'd been no one else there I'd have taken my own. But I wished I hadn't. There's no point knowing that someone's heartbeat is thin, thready and racing if there's nothing you can do about it.

I thought Costigian was going to start breaking things. A darkness emanated from him, a potential for violence, that filled the room and took up all the oxygen. Fear of him quivered in my veins. I had had kindness from this man, good nature and generosity, and I had never seen him use his strength except in our defence. But the savagery in his eyes now made all that seem like a dream.

Events had driven him from corner to corner and despite his best efforts had closed in round him. Like any animal hounded until it's trapped, he'd become dangerous. I don't know if his training had been different from Marion's or if it had just taken differently, like different fabrics taking dye. But he had no urge at all to get things down on paper. He wanted to kill someone. If they tried to take us by force, the first man through the door had better be armed with a flame-thrower.

'We don't even know why,' he snarled. 'They're killing us, and we don't even know why.'

The growing light revealed new details of our refuge. There was a telephone, but we knew better than to lift it – the line would go straight to Growth Industries. And there was water on tap, so we wouldn't need to catch the rain in a waste-paper bin. And there was an interconnecting door between the office and the shed.

It was locked, but it didn't stay locked for long. 'Mind the noise,' warned Marion, so Costigian kicked it through the towel that was hanging by the tap.

The smell rolled over us, crawling out of the shed like a great sluggish animal that had been confined there. Acrid fumes bit at the back of my throat and stung tears to my eyes, and I felt my knees wobble with the noxious gases dissolving in my bloodstream.

'Holy God!' gasped Costigian, throwing his sleeve up to his face. 'Somebody let some air in here.' Marion was closest. But, choking as we were, she wouldn't throw the door wide for fear of attracting attention. She opened it and both the windows just enough to let the dawn breeze in.

The worst of the miasma rolled through the office and out of the building, and after a minute or two the smell became tolerable. Partly, I suppose, we got used to it. A thick chemical brew, some of whose elements I could almost identify though it was thirty years since I had studied chemistry, it continued to sit on the tongue like the rancour of bad meat, but the grip on the throat had eased.

His face screwed up with distaste, Costigian moved slowly into the shed. One by one the rest of us followed.

The building was much as he'd described it – pipes, vats and instruments – but only from inside were you conscious of the sheer size of it, stretching away like a great steel box. Twenty-five years ago when this had been new it must have gleamed like a space-ship. The steel panels were dull now, the steel deck gritty with salt, but it was impossible to remain unimpressed by engineering on so gargantuan a scale.

Each of the four waste tanks was a drum eight metres across with a pressure lid like the hatch of a submarine. They marched in Indian file down the centre of the shed. They stood only a little above waist height, even on me, but then

136

these weren't the holding tanks, just the tops of them. The tanks themselves dropped through the deck to the seabed. No wonder the place smelled like an alchemist's outhouse.

Entering each vat at floor level was a pipe almost wide enough to crawl through. They'd marched side by side through the marsh and up the jetty and entered the building through a four-part arch; then they parted and made their way each to a separate tank. We could hear the muted roar of material moving along them even through the thick steel.

Each vat also had a second pipe that ran from the pressure lid to the outside wall, ending in a massive valve. The system seemed to be that the tanker locked hoses into those valves and pumped the waste into its holds. In view of the efforts that had been made to keep the chemicals apart thus far, I supposed they would go into four separate tanks and be carried away to wherever waste tankers went. It was an efficient means of handling toxic waste in quantities that would otherwise have posed an enduring problem.

Costigian was studying the instruments. There were sets of dials for each vat, like the engine monitors on an airliner. Some of them were red.

'I'm trying to work out when the next tanker's due.' He tapped a dial with a fingertip. 'If I'm reading them right, it's due now. They won't want the tanks full to bursting in case they get a week of bad weather when the tanker can't dock. If they couldn't pump any more waste, they'd have to stop production.'

I squinted at him. 'Is that good news or bad?'

He barked a gruff chuckle. 'Beats me. Could depend on whether the ship is owned by GI or just hired to do a job. If the skipper'll take us off, even if he hands us over to the police, it's good news. If he hands us over to GI, it's bad.'

'A ship's master is a serious professional. If he gets involved in anything shady, he loses his ticket. That's a hell of a gamble to take.'

Costigian nodded. 'Unless he's involved already, in which case the gamble is what'll come out if we get away.'

Oddly, in view of the fact that it was our lives we were discussing, I didn't seem to have his full attention. He was still looking at the instruments, his eyes ranging over the dials as if seeking something and not finding it, and his brow was puzzled. 'Why are there only four?'

'Four?' There must have been a couple of dozen dials and buttons and God knows what else.

'Four volume indicators, four flow indicators, four pressure gauges, four valve controls – four of everything.'

Patiently I pointed out the blindingly obvious. 'There are four tanks.'

He looked at them, not so much as if he hadn't noticed them before, more as if he'd only just got round to counting them. 'Yeah.' Understanding was like a slow dawn rising in his eyes. The effort of thinking had broken up the rage that was like a thrombosis in his mind and I could almost see the intelligence beginning to circulate again. The relief in his voice – because even a condemned man is relieved to know why – was almost like a smile.

'*That's* what this is all about. That's why they need us dead. There are four tanks. And there should be five.'

V

Fifth Column

Sixteen

Neither of us was shouting or waving our arms. I could see the light of revelation in Costigian's eyes but no one else could. Yet somehow, one by one, they became aware that what we were saying was important, and when I dragged my eyes off the Canadian's face and glanced round they were all there, listening to us in avid silence.

'There were five at the plant,' Costigian was saying. 'Remember – they had numbers on them? That little brick shed where we found the Transit – that was number 5. Those sheds are where the pipes go underground, so there are five pipes. But only four pipes arrive here and feed into four vats. What happens to the fifth one?'

'Maybe it's mixed in with one of the others,' I hazarded.

'Under the marsh?' There was a fine disdain in his voice. 'Any treatment of the waste would happen in the plant or here, not someplace in between. Five pipes leave Growth Industries and five ought to arrive here. But this building never held five tanks. There isn't room for another one.'

I shrugged helplessly, too tired to struggle with the paradox. 'Then where does the fifth pipe go?'

And the answer was that it didn't go anywhere. It went out into the marsh and there it ended. Three metres under the surface, out of sight and out of mind, an open-ended pipe had been gushing chemical toxins every day for quarter of a century. For quarter of a century Growth Industries had been paying for the disposal of only eighty per cent of the waste it generated. Every fifth year, effectively, there were no disposal costs. It was a massive commercial advantage – so significant that thirty years ago the plant had been designed around the idea. It was corporate crime on a huge scale, and

141

it must have involved every generation of the Wilson family since Emlyn had slipped his first backhander to an industrial architect.

Probably it was the lowest grade of waste that went untreated into the marsh. Probably he told himself it was big enough, and empty enough, to absorb the stuff. The only community close enough to be affected was Graveleigh, and it had been on the skids when the plant opened. In another ten years the place would be empty. Less, now Saul was dead.

All the same, Emlyn Wilson had been lucky. In twenty-five years the only evidence of what he'd done was in the shape of Saul Penny's back. His mother had known instinctively why he was born crooked, and now I knew too. She was one of the few who lived on The Island and worked at GI, and she walked across the marsh every day, winter and summer. The toxin that invaded her pregnancy was not something in the air but something in the water. Usually in summer the water table was low and the toxins deep in the marsh where they didn't do much harm. But in winter, and a wet summer like this one, they rose to the surface.

Which also explained why the Adventure School, though its students were prone to mild cold-like symptoms, hadn't suffered serious illness until now. The courses didn't run in winter, and in a normal summer the marsh would be drier. But we'd been splashing in and out of bog-holes since we got here. Nick had done the most splashing, and after him John. And John might have been all right, might have got better, except that he'd plunged into the black water when there'd seemed a chance Nick could still be alive.

Chase and Hollis suffered no symptoms because continual low-grade exposure to the toxin had developed in them a degree of immunity. And unlike Mrs Penny, they left in the autumn. But the bird-watchers who came in winter got ill just from squatting quietly in the wet fen for a day or two.

Well, Mrs Penny might have been unlucky and the bird-watchers might have caught chills, but there was no way the death of a healthy teenager was going to be shrugged off. An autopsy on Nick would reveal levels of toxic chemicals in his body that could only have come from Growth Industries, and the place would be shut down while the factory inspectorate went over it with magnifying glasses. Then the secret of the fifth pipe disgorging its noxious flood into the marsh would be out. And everyone at GI who'd ever known about it would face charges up to and including corporate manslaughter. No: after what happened to *Hereward* it would be murder.

And this was a fish that rotted from the head. Sir Emlyn – but he had been plain Mr Wilson then, a man of modest resources but big ideas – had designed not only his building but his whole commercial strategy around this lethal deceit. And he had brought his sons and his grandchildren into the firm because family were the only people you *could* trust with a secret like that. Probably no one else in the plant, now or in the past, had seen enough pieces of the puzzle to know what the secret of their success really was. They took their orders and did their jobs, and nobody whose surname wasn't Wilson was ever allowed to glimpse the whole picture.

The thing about rich, respected, important men is that they have a lot to lose. Emlyn Wilson knew, and Ernest Wilson knew, what would happen to them if the secret came out. Not much more would happen to them if it turned out that, alongside the lives they'd ruined and the unborn babies they'd condemned, they'd also killed people to protect their business and themselves.

I remembered my meeting with the company secretary in the corridor outside Donald Rodway's office – dear God, was it only twenty-four hours ago? I remembered the cool appraisal of his gaze. When he'd realized GI had finally made someone sick enough for the cause to be investigated, Ernest Wilson was already considering what to do about us. I think if Nick's life had depended on getting him to a hospital he'd still have died.

'The bastards!' said Marion, awestruck. But a kind of relief was audible in her voice. The danger was undiminished but at least we were free of that dreadful helpless confusion of being hunted for our lives and not knowing why. 'Did they expect to get away with it for ever?'

'Do *you* think they won't?' growled Costigian.

'What about Tom Chase?' But I knew I was scraping the bottom of the barrel.

Marion shook her head with regret. 'It's only a few miles: if he'd got through he'd have raised the alarm by now, there'd have been boats and helicopters looking for us at first light. And if he didn't get through . . .' She didn't bother to finish the sentence.

'But if we *all* go missing,' I whined, '*somebody's* going to ask questions!'

'Of course they are. But not at GI. Or at least, they'll ask and be told that we were there, took a shower and left. Nobody looking for us is going to take time to count the waste pipes.'

'They'll ask at Graveleigh. Mrs Penny . . .'

'Mrs Penny has to live there, and now she has to live there alone. She may decide that the only way is to know nothing.'

'But they killed her son!'

'I don't expect they'll tell her that. They'll tell her that *Hereward* broke up and sank. That it's our fault he's dead.'

Which raised another point. 'Are they still looking for us, do you suppose? Or do they think we died on *Hereward* too?'

Costigian's broad face was grim. 'You bet your sweet life they're still looking. They can't afford not to. The crew of the *Keith and Mary* saw Saul, no one else: not on the boat or in the water. They're looking, all right. And the fact that *Hereward* sank within sight of their jetty won't have escaped their notice.'

And of course he was right. As soon as the *Keith and Mary* docked in Graveleigh – sooner if whatever it was that was blocking the mobiles didn't affect her radio – someone would report to Ernest Wilson and he'd work it out. Allowing time for him to examine his conscience – say, a minute and a half – and issue fresh orders to his security team, we could expect our peace to be shattered any time now.

There was nothing to be done about it. With *Hereward* gone, the only way off the jetty was past the security hut and then past the plant. We could hope that while Wilson was marshalling his forces we'd be rescued by the waste

144

tanker, or a passing pleasure boat, or a division of Marines practising beach-head landings, but the odds weren't good.

The thoughtful quiet ended abruptly with the drilling of the telephone. We exchanged startled glances but no one moved to answer it. It rang half a dozen times, then fell silent. I said leadenly, 'They were bound to think of it sooner or later.'

'They may not take the fact that we're not answering as proof that we're not here,' Costigian suggested ironically. 'We need to decide what to do when they arrive. Do we go with them or make them take us?'

There wasn't much to be said for fighting, but nothing at all for giving in without a struggle. Time was the only ally we had. We agreed to hold them off as long as we could.

You know that sensation of having forgotten something? You check your diary, and under the phone where you leave notes when you can't find your diary; and then you check the fridge in case you needed to go shopping, and the TV papers in case it was a programme you wanted to watch; and after that you ask your husband, and he says frostily that it was his birthday? Well, that's the feeling I got right about then. I wandered back into the office, hoping something in there would remind me.

It did. What I had forgotten was that I was a doctor in charge of a very sick man.

Back in the shed I could hear voices as they continued discussing the endgame. After a minute George followed me into the office and closed the door quietly behind him.

'John?'

I looked up from where I sat on the floor with him, his wrist still limp between my fingers, and nodded. 'Yes.'

'Is he dead?'

'Yes.' The spiteful fates that had denied him a soldier's life had given him a soldier's death: messy and slow, without the appropriate care or dignity, and fifty years too soon.

We said nothing more, George and I. We just stayed with him for a while, taking our leave. There wasn't the same sense of grief as we'd felt yesterday when Nick had died. It wasn't that we'd thought any less of John. The difference was that Nick had been snatched from us when we'd thought he still had half a century's living to do. By the time John died, by any realistic assessment he'd only been robbed of a few hours.

So George stood by the door, like a sentry at the foot of a catafalque, and I sat on the floor by the dead man, absent-mindedly straightening his hair. I had a sense of being somehow *in loco parentis*. God knows I was no substitute for his mother, but I wanted his last dealings with the human race to be gentle. I stroked his hair as if I was putting a child to bed. After a little while I went back into the shed.

I'm not sure they'd missed me. Marion and Costigian were arguing again, this time over where and how an effective barricade could be built. I didn't bother listening: whatever they decided would make no difference. When they both paused for breath at the same time I said, 'We can't stay here.'

That got their attention. Marion's eyebrows arched upwards, Costigian's drew down. Marion snorted, 'We can't go anywhere else.'

But Costigian knew I had something important to say and waited for me to say it.

I drew a deep breath and got it out. 'John's dead. Well, that's not much of a surprise. But the reason we have to leave here is the reason he died now instead of an hour ago. What killed him was the fumes coming off those tanks. If we stay, they'll kill us too.'

Costigian looked at the tanks, and at the office door, and shook his head. His voice was low and his eyes scoured my face. 'That's crazy. People work in here all the time. The instruments . . .'

'No, people *don't* work here all the time. Somebody works here sometimes – maybe for only half an hour when the tanker's due. Maybe he wears a suit and a respirator. I don't know. But I do know we've all been exposed to the same toxins as Nick and John, and that we've all been affected. We're sick right now, it's just that we've got used to it, and anyway we've had more pressing things to worry about. But

146

look at us! Look at the colour of your skin. We could play *The Mikado* without make-up, for God's sake!'

I saw them startle, and look, and see. I wasn't even exaggerating. George looked like a ghost already. The whites of Costigian's eyes were the colour of marmalade.

'As long as we go on breathing these fumes we're going to get worse. Nick went down first because he swallowed more marsh water than the rest of us. We couldn't keep him out of it, remember? John was working harder and getting wetter than anyone else. The longer and more intense the exposure, the worse the symptoms. Jimmy'll be next, because most of the time Nick was playing mud-puppies Jimmy was too. After him, any one of us. Just for the record, my head's going like a trip hammer.

'Think about this. If you're right, we were poisoned by a dilute accumulation of the lowest grade of waste leaving the plant. Here we're camping next to a concentration of the most toxic waste they produce, stuff they didn't dare pump into the marsh. Hauling John up here on a rope didn't kill him. What came out when we opened the door did.'

It wasn't that they didn't believe me. I could see in the depths of their muddy eyes that they did. They just didn't know how to react. Marion explained, as if to a child, 'We can't leave. They're waiting for us.'

All I could do was repeat what I'd already said. 'If we stay, we're going to die.'

Costigian said savagely, 'It's your professional opinion, is it, that we'd be safer at Growth Industries?'

I shrugged. 'It's my professional opinion that we'd be as safe. It'll come to the same thing anyway. If we don't walk off the jetty today we'll be carried off tomorrow.'

He went on looking at me angrily, as if it was my fault. I didn't need that. I'd just lost my second patient in two days, two other people I'd come to think of as friends were dead, and it seemed only a matter of time before the Grim Reaper came for the rest of us. Also, I wasn't exaggerating about my head. I turned away wearily. 'Suit yourself. Like I say, it won't make much difference.'

Jimmy followed me back into the office. He stood just

inside the door, looking at the still form in the corner. There was nothing to cover him, so he looked more like a sleeper than a corpse. From the way Jimmy couldn't take his eyes off him, I guessed he'd never seen a dead man before.

Still without looking at me he said, 'Did you mean that? About me being next?'

There was no point lying. 'You started the symptoms soon after Nick, didn't you? I don't suppose the night you got lost in the marsh helped. So yes, maybe you'll be next. But it's academic now. We're none of us walking away from this.'

He dragged his eyes off John and flicked them at me like a frightened animal. His voice was shrill. 'How can you say that? How can you be so calm?'

I put out my hand and drew him to me, and he came reluctantly and sat beside me on the desk, his thin body rigid with fear. 'I'm not calm, I'm just knackered. I'm too tired and too sick to do a song and dance about it, that's all. I'm every bit as scared as you. We all are. But there's nothing more we can do.'

I had my arm about him. I think it gave him comfort; it certainly gave me some. 'You know something, Jimmy? We did pretty well with the crap hand we got dealt. We must have had them sweating in their Savile Row suits. We took all the chances we were given, we made some of our own, and if we'd had half the luck we were entitled to we'd have made it. We were a good team. You were part of a good team.'

The football hooligan in him managed to raise a smile. 'But we're not going to get a replay, are we?'

I squeezed him. 'We wuz robbed.'

Seventeen

There was no more talk of fighting at the barricades. We waited for them to come, listening for vibrations in the steel deck of the jetty, and for an hour we heard nothing. The sun, wrapped in the old dressing gown of cloud it had worn for so long, dragged itself up the sky as if it would really just as soon not bother, and I knew how it felt.

If there'd been anything left to fight for, headache or no headache I'd have been piling furniture behind the door. I was never good at waiting, and I wouldn't have been meekly waiting for men with murder in their eyes if there'd been any alternative that didn't involve watching my companions sicken and die. Whatever Wilson intended, I didn't think it would be worse than dying by inches.

The phone rang again. George looked at me and I shrugged. 'They know we're here.'

He picked it up with his good hand and said, 'Graveleigh Seaquarium, Mr C. Lyon speaking.'

I grinned. I admired humour – even puerile humour – from a man so weak he could hardly stand. But he wiped the grin off my face when he held it out. 'It's for you.'

'Clio? Dr Marsh? Thank God.' It was Donald Rodway and his voice was strident with anxiety. 'I called before. No one answered.'

'We were busy.'

He was hardly listening. 'Clio, you have to get away from there. It's dangerous.'

Now that *was* funny. 'Tell me about it.'

'The waste in the vats – it's toxic. Even the fumes are toxic. The men wear full protection to work there. I'm sending the bus to collect you.'

'We don't need a bus any more, Donald,' I said tiredly, 'there are only five of us left.'

I think that shocked him. 'What? How . . . ?'

'Saul's dead and John's dead, and I imagine Tom Chase is dead too. Wait a bit longer and you can pick us up with a wheelbarrow.'

The drilling of the phone had brought the others. But neither Costigian nor Marion asked to take the conversation over. They listened closely, Costigian bent over the desk like a bear fishing for salmon. I mouthed 'Rodway' and he nodded.

There was a pause then. I thought the doctor was conferring with someone. When he spoke again his voice had dropped a tone. 'Clio, you really don't sound well. You have to leave the terminal. You're going to make yourselves awfully ill if you don't.'

'Donald,' I said patiently, 'we *are* awfully ill. We're awfully ill, and some of us are dead, because when we tried to leave GI we were prevented. By your employers. Is there anything you can do to ensure us a safe passage this time?'

I knew I was wasting my breath, but at least he stopped preaching at me. He stammered out a sentence containing the words *misunderstanding* and *overreaction* and *talk about this*, then there was another hiatus. I could almost see Ernest Wilson leaning over his shoulder, telling him what to say.

'You're not making any sense, Clio. The stuff you're breathing has affected your ability to think. We're going to have to pull you out of there, whether you like it or not. Some people will come down to the jetty to fetch you. Please come peaceably.'

With a scowl, Costigian took the phone. 'Listen to me. You try flushing us out of here before we're ready and some things are going to get broken. Expensive things. But you're right about one thing – the place is killing us. We are going to have to talk. Wait half an hour. We'll get back to you.'

'You haven't got half an hour,' said Rodway. 'I'll see you in fifteen minutes.' He rang off.

While I was talking Costigian was thinking. Now he looked up with a new purpose in his yellow eyes. 'I have an idea. But we have to split up. Fletcher, take the others ashore.

150

This won't work if we're all together when they come. They'll know I won't blow the terminal up with you people still in it.'

You could have called it a gamble, or an act of despera-tion. In other circumstances you'd have accepted it as proof of insanity. But the situation we were in made a mockery of rational behaviour. Maybe this spawn of Costigian's dark side would achieve nothing, but it could hardly make matters worse. It's the upside of utter despair – that you have nothing to lose. Once your most fundamental rights have been wrested from you, there's nothing left to fear. It makes you a uniquely dangerous animal.

And with the fear go the inhibitions. It's like emptying your pockets of dozens of little lead weights. Social and legal strictures mean nothing to someone who doesn't expect to see tomorrow. Remember that, if you ever have it in mind to destroy someone. If you destroy his hope, make sure you destroy the man soon afterwards.

I couldn't imagine any other circumstances in which an officer of the Royal Canadian Mounted Police would be proposing to blow up a British industrial installation, and a British police officer, two other honest upright citizens and also Jimmy Ferris would be hearing him out. It was a measure of what we'd been reduced to, and also what we were capable of. Even the probability of failure hardly concerned us. It was something to try. It was better than dying like sheep.

'The main thing,' said Costigian, talking fast and low, 'is that we grab the initiative. I want the rest of you waiting at the shore when they come. Demand to see Wilson right away. Tell them to stay off the jetty if they value their skins.

'Tell Wilson that unless he lets you go it'll be Guy Fawkes night out here. There has to be something volatile in this lot. Or if I can't get it to burn, I'll open the valves and dump it. That should attract the kind of attention he's keen to avoid.'

I was nodding. Almost, I didn't care if it was a good plan or a bad one. It was a plan, and it felt good not to be running any more.

Costigian went on: 'Tell him that if you don't phone me inside two hours from a police station, I'll wipe his terminal out. Whether it's flames a hundred feet high or dead fish stinking up the Norfolk beaches, it'll be a trail leading straight back here. With or without us, the investigation will find his fifth pipe. He might as well let us go. His secret's out, and he doesn't need five more deaths to explain.

'But splitting up is the key to it. If I hold the terminal, he has to let you go. And once you're free, he has to let me go too.' He grinned fiercely. 'I think. I hope.'

All the time he was speaking, unfolding his plan in that low, urgent monotone, I was watching his face. Trying to work out from the expression in his eyes whether he understood the implications of what he was saying. And I thought he did.

Marion looked at him and thought he didn't. She was reluctant to burst the bubble but thought it was important to be realistic. 'I don't think Wilson will be that easy to bluff.'

He met her gaze. 'I'm not bluffing.'

'No, quite,' she agreed. 'We'll make it as convincing as we can. Maybe he'll feel he can't take the risk. But he's a cold-blooded sod to have done what he's done so far. What if he says, "Well, you can't make things any worse for me, go ahead and blow it up"?'

'I'll blow it up.'

'No, really. What do you do at that point?'

'Fletcher,' he said into her face, 'I'll blow it up. Or I'll dump it. A fire would be better. A fire will bring people faster than poisoned fish. Maybe fast enough to rescue you. If you can hold out for half an hour – lock yourselves in a room, hold them off with a power-hose, anything – just keep them at bay for thirty minutes after the fireworks start—'

'Costigian,' she interrupted in exasperation, as if he'd forgotten something vital. 'If you blow up the terminal, where will you go?'

The disbelief was etched in his face and for a second he was literally lost for words. I stepped in quietly to fill the breach. It was only at moments like this, when they were staring at one another in stunned silence, that I could get a word in edgeways. 'Marion – where do you *think* he's going?'

I saw the slow tide of comprehension creep through her,

her eyes grow appalled. 'But – that's *suicide*!'

He laughed out loud, with no mirth whatever. 'Yeah.'

'No.' She shook her head emphatically. 'There has to be some other way.'

'Like?'

'*I* don't know. But there must be. If we think . . .'

'We've been thinking,' he pointed out. 'Non-stop, for twenty-four hours. We thought of sending Chase across the marsh. That didn't work. We thought of sailing out on *Hereward*. That didn't work. We thought of hiding out in the terminal: now Dr Strangelove' – he meant me – 'tells me that won't work either. We're all out of options, Fletcher. I didn't say it was a great idea. It's just the best I can come up with.'

'No,' she said again. 'I can't allow it. I can't—'

He didn't let her finish. 'It isn't your call. I'm going to give it a try. If it works, we're free and clear.'

'And if it doesn't, you'll die in a chemical fire!' she cried. 'Can you imagine what that would be like?'

'I don't need to imagine it,' shouted Costigian furiously. 'I don't *want* to imagine it. I hope it won't come to that. But by God, if we're all going to die, I want to know somebody's going to pay for it! I'd rather go out with a bang than a whimper.'

Something in Marion's eyes was changing. She was still staring at him, white-faced, slack-mouthed with shock. But in the depths of her eyes intelligence stirred. 'I know why you're doing this,' she whispered. 'Because I'm here.'

'Don't flatter yourself,' sneered Costigian, turning away.

But she had seen into his soul and what she found there had stopped her racing thoughts short, like a running dog hitting the end of a long leash. She knew him now, had seen him where he lived, and she believed that he was offering himself as a blood sacrifice because of matters that were unresolved between them.

She couldn't let that pass. She followed him, manoeuvring to keep her face before him. 'Because of what happened at King's Cross. Because you misread the situation and a good man died. It was your fault: everyone who was there knew

153

it. Now you'll do anything – *anything*, however dangerous, however obscene, whatever the cost – rather than take responsibility for more innocent lives. If the only way is to kill yourself, you'll do that too.'

Her voice was rising, the anger vibrating in it like a guitar string. 'I know it's meant to sound brave and noble, but actually it's just a different kind of opting out. These people need help and guidance, Costigian, and you're an officer of the law and that *makes* you responsible for them. And maybe you can't save them. Maybe the best efforts of both of us won't be enough. But you owe it to them, and to the job, to try. Not to make them watch you die because it's easier than you watching them.'

He could ignore her jibes only so long: sooner or later he always rose to them. He rounded on her now, coals sparking in his eyes. I think if she'd been a man he'd have picked her up by her shirt-front. 'Fletcher, I don't care what you think of me. I don't care what your friends at the Met think. I'm sorry about your friend, but I didn't shoot him. Sure, with hindsight I made a mistake. But none of us, not even you, knew that at the time it was happening. That's not just me saying that: it's what the inquiry said. I have nothing to apologize for and nothing to prove.

'I've told you what I'm going to do. I think it's possible – no more than that – that I can save lives this way. If any of us survives, Growth Industries will pay. Even if none of us makes it, half the country's going to know *something* happened here and someone will find out what. It's hard to get much satisfaction out of your own death but yes, if I've got to die, I quite like the idea of bringing down the guy responsible. But in case you make it and I don't, I'd like you to know one thing: I'm not doing it to impress you.

'You're a good cop, Fletcher. Stick with it: you're a crap psychologist.'

They were spitting fire at one another again. I couldn't judge which of them was right about King's Cross, but I was pretty sure Costigian's proposal was the only chance we had. He knew what he was doing. He knew the price he'd pay if it didn't come off. What drove him on was an absolute refusal to be beaten.

I linked my arm through Marion's and steered her away. 'Let's get the others. We have to be away from here before Rodway comes.'

She hung back, staring at me incredulously. 'What are you saying? That he's right?'

'Of course he's right. We have to try to survive. The dead can't bear witness. If we stay together, we'll die together. See if George'll let you help him – he'll never make it down the jetty on his own.'

I steered her into the office and left Costigian standing alone in the shed, and when I turned to close the door he looked . . . abandoned. He'd won the argument, got his own way; we were doing as he said, leaving him alone in the terminal. It was victory of a kind. But when he thought no one was looking he let the hard tough impervious-to-all-known-corrosives policeman's patina slip and beneath it he looked sick and afraid. I said nothing. Even wishing him luck would have been impertinent. I closed the door quietly behind me.

We walked the length of the jetty. We didn't talk much. Jimmy looked back a couple of times, then asked timidly when Costigian was coming. I lied and said I didn't know.

They were waiting for us at the security hut. Rodway had brought his car. There were also four men in the black leathers of the security corps. We were barely outnumbered but it made no difference. We were no longer in any shape either to fight or flee.

Fifty metres from the hut, as if by common consent, our steps slowed and we ground to a halt, looking at our shoes and the steel plates of the deck and only briefly, as if embarrassed, at one another. It was like the waiting room of a VD clinic: we all knew what we were doing there but nobody liked to mention it.

Finally Marion said, 'God damn it, Clio, I can't leave him there alone. I'm going back.'

I stared at her, my brain so dulled I wasn't sure I'd understood. 'Back? You can't. You know what . . . what could happen. And he won't thank you.'

She managed a jerky laugh. 'Of course he won't. He's a man – and a policeman, and a foreign policeman at that. He was born to hate my guts. All the same, for lots of reasons, the terminal's where I should be. He's right: it's our last chance. We can't leave it in the hands of one man. One sick man.'

'And you're *not* sick?'

She grinned. 'Of course I'm sick. But not as sick as him. If I can stay on my feet an hour longer than him I can improve the chances of this working by maybe fifty per cent.'

I hesitated to say it out loud. But she deserved to know. 'You do realize that the bluff may not work. That in the end the terminal may have to be sacrificed. Costigian will do it if he has to.'

'Oh yes.' There was a weary little sorrow in her voice: I wasn't telling her anything she didn't already know. 'And if he won't, I will.'

I believed her. I believed she was right, that she could improve our chances. And I didn't suppose it mattered all that much where any of us was: if GI thought it could protect itself by killing us, we'd all die. But I didn't have to like it. 'That means I'll have to deal with Wilson!'

'Just make sure he understands that we're serious. That's all you can do. It's up to him what happens after that.' With a fey smile she turned and began to walk back the way we'd come.

I pushed George and Jimmy ahead of me like a mother hen rounding up a pair of gangling goslings. 'OK, let's move. We don't want them coming on to the jetty.' Hearts and limbs like lead, we stumbled towards the shore.

Rodway's eyes were deeply troubled, darting between me and Marion's receding back as if he had no idea what to do about her. 'Where's she going?'

'She forgot something,' I said brusquely. 'Don't waste my time. I have to talk to Wilson, now.'

'But . . .' He looked unhappily after the dwindling figure.

'Where do you think she's going to go?' I demanded roughly. 'Leave one of your men to bring her up to the plant when she's ready. Only you'd better warn him to wait here for her, not to go after her.'

'Why?'

I smiled coldly. 'Because we've booby-trapped the terminal, that's why.' The look of horror in his face was the only good thing that had happened today. I climbed into the back of his car and eased George in beside me. 'Oh, come on, Donald. I promise, if it blows up, you'll be the first to know.'

Eighteen

S till, after all that had happened, Donald Rodway refused
to believe we were facing death. He wasn't a stupid man,
he wasn't an evil man. He seemed genuinely unable to
comprehend that there were people in the world – in his
world, people that he passed in corridors and met in the
canteen – who would purpose the destruction of other human
beings for profit.

So I asked how he supposed we had dwindled from the
number we had once been to what we were now, and when
he shrugged awkwardly I took a certain macabre pleasure
in telling him. He knew about Nick, of course, and about
George's shoulder. He didn't know about Chase, lost in the
marsh; about Saul, run down by the *Keith and Mary*; about
John, choking his life out as GI's poison worked its corro-
sive way in him. He grew pale with the telling.

And still he fought against belief. He thought I'd got it
wrong. He was appalled that Chase had tried to cross the
half-remembered fenland track at night. And John should
never have been taken to the terminal. He had been ill before
we left GI: whatever was I thinking of to take him to a chemical dump? As for the loss of *Hereward*, he thought that must
have been an accident. It was barely daylight when it had
happened: after a night's fishing the trawler might have been
keeping a careless watch. It was a tragedy someone would
have to answer for, but blaming GI was sheer paranoia.

I gave up. The facts meant nothing to a man that convinced
of universal human decency. If he'd found me dead in
Wilson's office with a knife in my back, he'd have thought
it had gone off while I was cleaning it. Almost, I felt sorry
for him. He wasn't one of the Wilson family retainers, hadn't

been there long enough for his loyalty to be counted on. When the immediate problem had been dealt with, I thought the company secretary would look long and hard at his medical officer.

I didn't have to ask for Wilson again: I was taken to his office as soon as we reached the plant. Alone: somewhere between the foyer and the clinic my security escort – it was Gallagher again, instantly recognizable without his helmet – steered me round a corner while my companions went straight on. I paused and would have gone back for them, but Gallagher's hand in my back kept me moving forward. I could have yelled. It seemed a bit late in the day for that.

When we reached the secretary's office, Gallagher knocked, opened the door and propelled me inside. Then he closed the door and, I had no doubt, placed his back against it.

'Come in, Dr Marsh. Sit down.' Ernest Wilson was not alone. The big chair behind the desk was occupied by an older man, possibly around seventy, with enough silver-white hair to coax it into a dashing wave. He was slightly – not unhealthily – florid where his son was monochrome, but there was no missing the family resemblance.

'Sir Emlyn Wilson, I presume?'

He didn't offer his hand: he knew I'd ignore it. Instead he smiled confidently. 'I've been hoping to meet you.' The least trace of a Welsh accent survived in his voice.

'Really? Well, we were here long enough yesterday morning. Perhaps you should have made a little more effort.'

The surprise – he wouldn't deign to feel shock – of being addressed without respect travelled through his face like the pressure wave from a slap. But he said nothing, merely leaned back from the table. As if his disfavour should be punishment enough.

I did – I confess it – the most offensive thing I could think of. I gave a dismissive chuckle. 'I'm not here to socialize. I'm not here to negotiate. I've brought an ultimatum. Either you set us free or you'll lose your terminal, and with it any chance of keeping what you're doing here under wraps.'

Ernest Wilson was regarding me not like a threat, not like

159

a victim, perhaps like a blot on his ledger. An untidiness, something that shouldn't have happened, that would need sorting out. 'You imagine you know what we're doing here?'

It hardly mattered whether we did or not, only that we knew he was doing something he shouldn't be, and as the dead piled higher we'd have needed Rodway's faith in human nature to blame it all on luck. But if we'd worked it out from the evidence available to us, he'd know that qualified investigators would expand on that until they knew not only what he'd done but what he'd tried to do and what he'd thought of doing. The sooner the Wilsons understood that they were going to pay for what they'd done in the past, what they were doing right now and anything they did in the immediate future, the better.

I said, 'The rain was your undoing. It washed the toxins to the surface when they should have been safely locked away in the bottom of the marsh. It was bound to happen sooner or later. You shouldn't have encouraged Chase to run his survival courses over your secret dump.'

Emlyn Wilson angled bushy white eyebrows in a kind of facial shrug. 'On the contrary, it was a useful control. We made our doctor available so we'd know of any sickness among the students. There really didn't seem to be a problem: runny noses, the odd cough – only what you'd expect of people playing in a bog. We were confident that any increase in toxicity would affect the survivalists before it affected anyone else.'

He left me open-mouthed. I knew he was a ruthless man: until that moment I hadn't realized just how ruthless. What happened to us wasn't an accident, a freak event caused by abnormal weather conditions. It was what was meant to happen. We'd been used as miners used canaries: they knew there was firedamp around when the birds died. We'd been part of the early-warning system designed to protect Growth Industries from the consequences of its economies.

I tried to tell myself it altered nothing, but actually it did. Emlyn Wilson had known this would happen sooner or later. He would have made contingency plans.

Father and son, they went on watching me, waiting for a

reaction. But I had nothing to say, so after a minute I shut my mouth.

Ernest smiled a polite grey accountant's smile. 'You said something about the terminal?'

I wasn't prepared for this. Ten minutes ago I had thought Marion would be conducting this interview and it had seemed reasonably straightforward. It might not work, but the pitch itself was simple. Now suddenly it had got complicated. I had to convince these intelligent, calculating, above all unsurprised men that Costigian would do what he threatened, and that when the terminal went into meltdown their comfortable, profitable lives would too.

And all their instincts would be telling them I was wrong – that nothing a few sick people could work out in a few desperate hours would be clever enough to upset years of careful planning. From the moment he'd planned for five pipes going into the marsh and only four emerging, Emlyn Wilson must have known this moment would come. Must have known that getting it wrong would result in – depending on how much damage had been done by then – massive fines, the loss of the business or the wholesale removal of his family to jail. He had to have decided what he'd do before the first digger carved the first trench.

The only thing he couldn't have expected was the presence in his canary cage of two experienced police officers. All right: and me. Between us we had a range of skills that had already given him more problems than he'd ever anticipated. Was it worth hoping that we'd managed to frighten him, that behind that confident exterior he was worried what more we could achieve and open to a negotiated ceasefire before there were deaths on the charge sheet that even an expensive lawyer couldn't plead as accidental? I didn't think so. I still had to try.

I said quietly, 'It's over. You *know* it's over. You know the authorities are coming in here with every industrial specialist they can find, and when they leave they'll know everything you did and everything it cost. I'm not just talking about the lives of a bunch of survivalists. I'm talking about turning a bit of England's green and pleasant into Death

161

Valley. You have to know you're not walking away from that. Everyone who was in on it, and that's three generations of your family, is facing charges of corporate manslaughter. And we're not talking a momentary lapse here, approving the wrong amendment while the port's going round the boardroom table. We're talking about a deliberate and elaborate criminal deception. Let's put it this way: don't buy a Christmas tree this year.'

Neither of them demurred. But they weren't putting their swords on the table just yet either. I went on.

'So what you want to know is what you stand to gain by letting us go. It's simple. Corporate manslaughter is a big, big deal with big penalties for those convicted. But murder is bigger. Your grandchildren may in time live down the fact that their expensive lifestyle was funded by the rape of half a county, but conspiracy to murder will remain with them always. If this stops now, the price can probably be paid by you two. If it doesn't, no one in your entire family will escape the net. Now do you want to talk?'

I saw – or thought I saw: I had too much riding on this to be unbiased – flickers in the expressions of both men that suggested they were at least thinking about it. Never mind hearts and minds: if you want a man's undivided attention, grab him by the reproductive organs. I had put their children into the pot. It raised the stake incalculably. The florid man went a little redder, the grey man a little greyer.

Emlyn Wilson said roughly, 'I will not be blackmailed by a writer of penny-dreadfuls who claims the moral high ground and then threatens my grandchildren!'

But Ernest said quietly, 'Father. She's doing what she can. You can't blame her for that.'

'She'll destroy the family!'

'This is what you risked when you took the course you did nearly thirty years ago. I'm not criticizing you. I'm just saying, you can't blame a cornered dog for biting.' He looked at me. 'What exactly do you want?'

At least I knew the answer to that. 'I want to walk out of here with those of my friends who are still alive.'

'And for that, can we count on your silence?'

It was a trap. If I'd said yes, he'd have known he couldn't believe a word I said. 'That isn't an option. People have died; and two of the survivors are police officers. You can't avoid legal consequences. What you can do is limit the scope of them. Or pack a quick bag and whistle up an executive jet.'

Ernest was nodding slowly. 'I see. Well, you'll understand that we have to consider this. We'll let you know our decision.' As if I was asking him for a job.

I didn't think I'd done enough. I had to fight the urge to plead with him. 'You really don't have much time. I have to phone Costigian from a police station in not much more than an hour or he'll put a match to your terminal.'

A tiny smile hovered in the back of the secretary's eyes. 'He's a police officer – admittedly, a Canadian one. He's not going to devastate a significant portion of East Anglia to make a point. Any damage we may have done with our small economy would be swamped by the fallout from a fire at the waste terminal.'

I made myself shrug. 'He's not interested in making a point, and the only people he's thinking about right now are us. He will do it. For a good man he's a ruthless sod.'

He smiled openly at that. His father went to speak again, but Ernest stilled him with a fractional movement of his hand. He showed me to the door, returning me to Gallagher outside. 'We'll give it the most serious consideration,' he promised. 'This gentleman will show you where you can wait.' It was a dismissal. If I hadn't gone then, he'd have pushed me.

I hoped to be reunited with George and Jimmy, or failing that to be taken to the clinic. Only because it was a place I was familiar with. I'd given up hoping that Rodway would help. He couldn't afford to believe what I was telling him about his employers. Believing meant he'd have had to choose whether or not to help us. It was easier, and safer, to think that the whole thing was a figment of our marsh-fevered imaginations. So it wasn't his help I wanted so much as his company. However quickly the Wilsons came up with an answer, it would be a long wait alone.

163

But alone was what I got, locked in an empty storeroom on a little-used corridor with a small window higher than I could see out of. I had no way of knowing if my friends were in an adjacent room or half the plant away.

Twenty minutes dragged by, each composed of sixty flaccid seconds hauling bags of wet cement. In the blind room where I could see nothing I listened: with my ears and my skin and the tips of my fingers. I listened for feet in the corridor. And I listened for a sound like the end of the world rolling across the marsh from the terminal. If Emlyn Wilson thought it was a bluff, he'd call it. He'd round up every employee he could spare and have them rush the jetty. And Costigian wasn't bluffing. So I listened and listened, and heard nothing beyond the wind and the rain.

Then the door opened and I hadn't even heard the feet. It was Ernest Wilson. His narrow face was still, closed in. 'I'm sorry. It's not good news.'

He broke it like a doctor: quietly, unemotionally, with an explanation but no frills. 'My father and I have discussed the situation. We believe we've found a solution. Unfortunately, it depends on the absolute discretion of all who know about the fifth pipe, and that's the kind of loyalty you can only expect from family. I'm afraid, therefore, that we cannot accede to your request and let you go.'

I blinked. Of course I'd known it was a possibility. I'd managed to convince myself that it wouldn't happen – that he'd have to admit defeat. I swallowed, looking for a voice. 'I really wasn't kidding, you know. Costigian and Marion Fletcher will blow the terminal. They'll blow it if anyone tries to rush them, and they'll blow it anyway if they haven't heard from me in another forty minutes. They've nothing left to lose, and they'll do it.'

'I'm sure you're right,' he said. 'In fact I'm counting on it.' My lips formed a question mark. But before I could voice it he was speaking again. 'We did well to get away with it for twenty-five years. Now it seems the risks of continuing are starting to outweigh the benefits. If the toxins in the marsh have reached a concentration capable of causing serious illness, there's a limit to how much longer we can keep the secret. Quite apart from the present problem, we have to reorganize our waste disposal.'

I wasn't going to argue with that. 'Good . . .'

'The difficulty,' he went on, 'is that the major construction work involved could start people wondering why. It would be unfortunate to escape detection for twenty-five years only to arouse suspicion by putting things right. Happily, your Canadian friend seems to have provided us with the answer. The accidental destruction of the terminal would obviously mean rebuilding. It would also explain any contamination found in the marsh, now and for years to come. Once we connect up the fifth pipe no one will ever guess that it didn't originally reach the jetty. And even if they did, with the terminal building scattered across a square mile of seabed it would be hard to prove anything.'

He smiled – gently, sadly, a shade apologetically. If I'd felt inclined to cry he'd have offered me his perfectly laundered handkerchief. But that was all that was on offer. He was informing me of a decision, not engaging me in a debate.

I didn't feel inclined to cry. 'So you're going to kill us and let Costigian blow up the terminal.'

'Yes. If he'll do it. If he has second thoughts, we'll help.' He saw me staring and did the smile again, wintry grey. 'It's too important to depend on whether a Mountie finally gets angry enough to blow himself up.

'You may have noticed that the vats are almost full. There's a tanker due in this morning. If the terminal's still there when it arrives, there'll be a most unfortunate accident The tanker docking a little too quickly, perhaps – gas leaking from a valve – sparks . . .' He shrugged. 'Accidents do happen. And always – have you noticed? – at the worst possible time.

'It's a spectacular sight, of course, a tanker coming in. When people express an interest in watching, we're happy to accommodate them. It's just a pity that our kindness on this occasion is going to cost the lives of an entire intake of survivalists, both instructors, and even our own doctor, who offered to show them round.'

Nineteen

When he'd gone I retired to a corner of the room and sank to the floor. The game was over and we'd lost. Not for lack of trying: we'd been defeated by bad luck, bad health and the Machiavellian brain Ernest Wilson hid behind that characterless grey. We'd fought him with every weapon we could find, every idea we could formulate, and we'd lost.

Morality aside, he deserved to win. He'd been cleverer than us. In the end, for all our efforts, for all our willingness to fight at his level – to die, if die we had to, writing his name in blood and fire regardless of how much damage we might do and who else might suffer – we had played into his hands. We had provided him with the means of killing us, of silencing even the testimony of our dead bodies, of destroying the evidence of quarter of a century's lethal fraud. When the experts who would visit Growth Industries in the coming weeks took samples from the marsh, they would find only what they expected. Of course there was a massive escape of toxins from the waste system when one end of it went up in smoke.

An explosion at the terminal covered all the bases. There was no longer any reason to keep us alive. Any time now we'd be heading back to the jetty – in plastic bags: we'd be less trouble that way and there wouldn't be enough pieces left afterwards to autopsy.

Two hours, Costigian had said. He'd blow the terminal if we weren't safe in two hours. But he wouldn't. He'd wait until there was no hope left. Which was a pity. If the thing went up before the tanker arrived, maybe Wilson's plan would go off at half-cock. If the police and the fire brigade and the health and safety people got here before he'd had time to deal with us . . .

166

I realized with a shudder what it was I was hoping for: that Costigian would kill himself and Marion in time to save me. Catching myself thinking like that did nothing for my self-esteem. So I thought about Harry. About the big, comforting size of him – bigger and more comfortable with every year that passed. My husband likes classic cars. He rolls underneath them on something like a skateboard to inspect their plumbing. A while back he put smaller wheels on this thing. Then he replaced the wheels with castors, and now he was planning an inspection pit. The time was coming when he'd have to shift his attention to classic lorries with enough room under them for mechanics with middle-aged spread.

And I wouldn't see it. I wouldn't see his hair fall out. I wouldn't see him holding the paper further and further away while insisting he didn't need glasses. I'd embarrassed him at our last police ball by doing the funky gibbon while all the other wives were waltzing. And next time ACC Crime complimented him on his work, there'd be no one he could tell who would share his pleasure and not think he was boasting.

I sat hunched in a corner of the bare room, in the dim light filtered by rain on the small high window, and missed him, and resented more than I can say the fact that I wasn't going to see him again for the rest of my life.

This time I heard the footsteps hurrying up the corridor, and wrenched myself to my feet because I wouldn't have them find me crouched in a corner as if with fear. The lock turned and the door flew open, and it wasn't Wilson or Gallagher who'd come for me but Terry Hollis.

He was in a hurry, spared me only a brief look. He'd aged ten years. Shock was embedded in his eyes too deeply ever to come out. I didn't know how much he knew of what was going on, what was going to happen, but he'd seen something that shook him to his soul. He was not the same man he had been even this time yesterday.

He said, 'Quickly,' and held the door for me.

A dozen questions lined up in my brain. One got as far as pursing my lips, but on reflection I said nothing. He wasn't here to kill me and for the moment that was enough. I went with him, trotting to keep up.

There was a staircase. He stopped when he came to it. 'Do you know where the others are?'

I took a deep breath. 'Two are dead, two are on the jetty. George and Jimmy are here somewhere but I don't know where. We shouldn't waste time looking. They're both sick, I doubt we can do much for them.'

'You want to leave them?' His rough voice soared.

Reddening – or at least turning orange – I tried to explain succinctly. 'They can't leave here. George can barely walk. Their only chance is if we can raise the alarm quickly.'

'The phones are still out,' he said. 'I tried them.'

That surprised me. 'You did?'

He looked at me with dislike. 'Why do you think I'm here?'

'I don't know,' I said honestly. 'I take it something changed after you knifed Costigian.'

He didn't care what I thought of him. 'They killed Tom.'

I had thought this powerful young man cared for nothing beyond his own best interests. But I was wrong. He cared about Tom Chase – as a partner and as a friend. That was the horror in his eyes: that he'd ended up on the opposite side to Chase, and that his new partners had murdered his old one.

I knew by now that he hadn't got through the marsh. I hoped he'd been captured, thought he might have drowned. 'What happened?'

'I heard them talking as they brought him in.' We were standing beside the stairs, wasting time we could ill afford, but he wanted to tell me and I wanted to hear. 'They didn't see me. He almost made it – he got through the marsh, they caught him on the road and brought him back to Wilson. Like dogs retrieving a stick.

'And Tom . . .' He stopped and swallowed. His voice was low and flat, with that peculiar superficial numbness that grows like a membrane over emotions too powerful to deal with. 'He was fine. I saw him, I heard him talking. He was all right. Then first thing this morning Wilson told me he was dead. That they'd found him in a sink-hole the way we found Nick. He showed me the body.'

Finally he looked at me, his eyes stretched with anguish. 'They must have taken him outside and drowned him.'

I couldn't think what to say. He was in pain, but so was I and I deserved it less. I fell back on practicalities. 'Do they know you know?'

He shook his head fitfully. 'I don't think so. I was too stunned to say anything.'

If Wilson had suspected, he'd have had Hollis under lock and key too. Of course, the moment I was missed he'd know who was to blame, but right now I was free and I had an ally who wasn't suffering from marsh fever. It was better than I'd hoped for ten minutes ago.

I still wasn't thinking of escape. The only chance for any of us lay in sending up the balloon before Wilson was ready. We had to blow up the terminal, and we had to do it now.

My first thought was to send Hollis. He still enjoyed some freedom of movement, and he could jog to the jetty in the time it would have taken me to walk to the gate. But Costigian wouldn't trust anything he said. Hollis had joined the enemy. However much he insisted that I'd sent him, Costigian would believe his message came from Wilson. And while they were arguing, the tanker would be getting nearer.

'Don't ask me how,' I said, 'but you have to get me out of here and down to the jetty. Now – it can't wait. Can you do it?'

It was a direct appeal to his professional pride and he answered, 'Yes,' before he'd even wondered how. But this was what it was all about: the commando training, the life-and-death games. The basic precept of survival training is that people who are tough, fit and adaptable survive when people who aren't perish. Terry Hollis was strong enough and fit enough for both of us. His body was a finely tuned machine and this was what it was tuned for. He'd never have a better chance to show what it could do.

We could probably have left by the front door. Not everyone at GI was part of the conspiracy – most of them thought they were making fertilizer. A few of them thought they were

169

helping Wilson pull the wool over the government inspector's eyes. But only the Wilson family, only the top echelon of management, understood that what they were really doing was destroying lives for money.

Even so, we wouldn't have got far before Gallagher's men stopped us. But Hollis knew a way. He'd worked in security here, knew the weak spots. Perhaps he'd thought, pacing these corridors during the quiet hours of some early morning, that he was watching for the likes of me. Industrial spies come in all shapes and sizes. He could never in his wildest dreams have thought that one day he'd need to escape from the place himself.

Moving quickly and quietly we went up the stairs, along another corridor and through a storeroom on the edge of the processing area. The rumble of machinery shook the walls and the floor. Then Hollis pushed through a set of swing doors on to another flight of steps. To my surprise he went up again, not down, but only as far as the half-landing where the stairs turned.

Then I saw what he intended. 'Oh no,' I said with certainty.

It was a window. Not a big window – just enough to light the stairs. And not barred or bolted, because we were a good three storeys above ground level. To reach that window an intruder would have to climb up the outside of the building. If we went through it, we'd have to climb down.

Hollis gave me a tight smile. 'It's not as bad as it looks. There's a fire escape about four metres away.'

Four metres? An orangutan might have made it, swinging between arms on which the force of gravity had played for millions of years. But evolution had sent me down a different path. You rarely see a suburban housewife swinging through the trees these days, even in Skipley. I could no more have spanned four metres of high wall than I could have flown.

Hollis added, 'And there's a ledge.'

I looked at him much as Adam must have looked at God when He was talking airily about borrowing a rib. 'How big a ledge?'

'A *wide* ledge,' he said firmly. 'You won't fall. I won't let you fall.' So I looked.

He'd exaggerated. It wasn't a ledge, it was a bit of decorative moulding. Maybe a cat could have inched along it, as long as it didn't look down, but I didn't think a human being could do it even to save his life. 'No way!'

Was it the Blarney Stone bestowed on Terry Hollis the gift of honey-tongued persuasion? 'Then stay here, because that's the way I'm going.'

He went first so that I could watch him, see how he did it, how easy it was. Also, if we were surprised and I froze there, at least I wouldn't block his escape.

The ledge may have been a little wider than it looked. He stepped on to it from the window sill and sidled along, face to the wall, his cheek against the bricks. He spread his arms wide and, rather than jamming his toes into the wall, let his heels hang over the edge, keeping his centre of balance forward. A little like a crab, a little like a crucified saint, he inched along the ledge.

My heart was in my mouth, but I needn't have worried. This was his world: he knew how to deal with this kind of danger. Corporate fraud, profit-and-loss murder – these were things beyond his comprehension. But pitting his strong young body against forces of nature like gravity and vertigo and fear – this he understood. In less than a minute he reached the fire escape. His reaching hand closed on the rail and he turned quite casually and stepped over the yawning gulf on to the treads. He was safe.

And he was four metres from where I sat quaking on the window sill. 'Your turn,' he said, stretching out his hand.

He was a tall man, his reach correspondingly long. But from where I was to where he could grab me was still an awfully long way. I shook my head. 'I can't do it.' The words came out in a fast stammer like machine-gun fire.

He looked genuinely surprised. 'Of course you can. Pretend it's the climbing wall.'

'I couldn't *do* the climbing wall!'

He'd forgotten. 'Well, this is easier. You don't have to climb, just shuffle. Plus, you don't have any choice.'

That about summed it up. If I fell, I would die – but also if I didn't take the risk of falling. I had nothing to lose. The ledge at least offered a chance. I swung my legs over the sill and looked at them dangling three storeys above the tarmac. Then I swung them back inside.

Hollis mistook this for a rational decision. 'That's right, keep your face to the building. Now hold the window frame and stand up on the sill.'

That much I managed because by looking through the window I could half-convince myself that I was still indoors. I knew my backside was swinging over an abyss, but still I was only just outside. I could go back in any time I wanted.

'Now stretch your left arm along the wall towards me. Feel the bricks with your forearm and the inside of your elbow.' That too I could do without releasing my death-grip on the window frame. I felt the wet roughness through my sleeve.

Dear God, if the bricks were wet, the ledge was wet! All the rain hitting that high wall would pour down over the ledge. It had been wet for months: there would be moss and algae waiting to shoot me over the edge. It wasn't possible . . . it wasn't *reasonable* . . .

'Good,' came Hollis's voice, remorselessly encouraging. 'Don't let go of the frame, not yet. But you need to get your left foot on to the ledge. Take your time. Feel for it with your toe, find a position you're comfortable with. That looks good. How does it feel?'

Someone had moved my foot out on to the ledge. My right was still on the sill and my knees began to tremble.

'Now your body.'

There's not a lot of me out front. I've always been able to buy bras from the Back to School range. But in order to squeeze past the window frame I had to lean out from the wall. The sweat was pouring under my clothes.

One thing about swinging in space: the ledge felt more substantial afterwards than it had before. I laid my hot cheek against the rough brick and felt almost safe.

'Keep coming,' said Hollis. So I did. Three inches at a time. With my heart hammering in my ears, and my face burning, and my back cold with the driving rain and sweat in my hair, I did as he said.

172

'OK, good. Now, don't look down.'

He shouldn't have said that. I hadn't wanted to look down. But now my eyes kept trying to creep away from the wall and over my shoulder.

'No, *don't* look down,' snapped Hollis.

I managed another three shuffles, then I looked down.

I didn't so much freeze as melt. My muscles softened, the strong fibres turning to string. My shoulders slumped, my palms slipped down the wall and my knees started to bend, projecting my posterior further into space.

A torrent of abuse from the fire escape shocked some rigidity back into my wilting structure. 'Oh you *stupid* bloody woman! Why do I *always* get the morons? I *told* you not to look down. Well, fall – see if I care. I'll be quicker on my own anyway. Of course, this vital message you have for Costigian is going to explode all over the tarmac when you do. What the hell, I don't expect it matters.'

Indignation and a renewed sense of purpose stiffened the sinews and summoned up a bit of blood. I crept back up the wall. I think I left some of the skin of my cheek on it. When I was erect again, I resumed shuffling.

Three metres from where I had let go the window frame to where he could get a hand to me. It felt both more and less than that. In the doing it was one of those nightmares of endless endeavour, of striving and striving and achieving nothing, of running in treacle or labouring under a heavy load. But then, almost before I was expecting it, my Zimmer-frame technique of sliding one foot three inches, then following with the other, brought me to the rail of the fire escape. I felt Hollis's strong grip on my elbow, and with me climbing and him hauling I got over the rail and collapsed in a heap on the wet steps.

I dashed the rain and sweat from my eyes and looked back. Four metres. One stride for a cantering horse. A couple of beds laid end to end. Nothing.

I looked up at Terry Hollis, and he was all grin. I panted indignantly, 'And if you *ever* speak to me like that again . . . !'

And he kissed me.

Twenty

The gate that habitually stood open, that even in the middle of the night was incapable of keeping a feverish boy from wandering off to his death, was open still. So no one had yet realized I was at large. If he'd known, the first thing Ernest Wilson would have done was lock it, because there was only one and – short of either digging under the ten-foot fence or scrambling over it – we had to go through it.

Not that our problems would end at the perimeter. Wilson had told me he intended to have me killed: sooner or later – and in all the circumstances sooner was safer – someone was going to go into that storeroom to do it. He'd find me gone, he'd raise the alarm, and within a couple of minutes Ernest Wilson would have the ATVs heading at top speed for the jetty. Even an optimist, which I never had been even before this week, wouldn't have thought there was time to spare.

It was half a mile from the plant to the jetty. Normally I could have walked it in ten minutes. Feeling as I did now, partly with reaction that might pass but also with the chemicals in my blood, I'd need to add VAT. With Hollis's help I could get through the gate even if the watchman raised a challenge. What we couldn't do was stay ahead of the entire GI security corps mounted on ATVs and armed with monkey wrenches.

No one knew of any reason why Hollis shouldn't be wandering round the compound. He took advantage of the fact and strolled past the gatehouse, then strolled back to me. There was only one man on guard, and he had his feet on the desk and was reading the sports pages of a tabloid newspaper. I imagine he had been doing pretty much the same thing the night Nick died.

174

Hollis said, 'We'll have to split up. You go on, I'll stay here, keep this chap quiet. At the first sign of trouble I'll lock the gate. I probably can't stop them, but I bet I can slow them down plenty.'

'There'll be more security down at the jetty.'

'You'll have to talk your way past them. Hey, Clio, there's a stroke of luck – the one thing you're better than anybody else at!'

Finally we looked at one another – me looking up, him down – without antagonism, without affection either, but with respect.

'Good luck,' I said, and he nodded.

'You too.'

As an afterthought I added, 'If they get hold of you, don't let them bring you to the jetty.'

His eyes widened but he nodded. 'OK. Why?'

'Just don't. Trust me on this.'

Though I was standing right beside the gatehouse when he slipped inside, I heard nothing. No raised voices, no sounds of a struggle – nothing. But I saw the shadow of the security guard vanish, and when it reappeared it was a size bigger and adjusting its peaked cap. And I was on my way.

The temptation was to run as fast as I could. But I was going to be out on the flat marsh alone for fifteen or twenty minutes: my only chance of avoiding capture was to look, at least from a distance, like a pipe-tapper, and I was pretty sure they never ran anywhere.

So I shuffled down the track with an odd combination of nonchalance and speed, and the rain beat at my face but also at the windows between me and anyone watching. At first I walked with my shoulders tense and my hackles up, waiting for the alarm. But none came, and when I stole a backward glance the gate was still open and there was no movement in front of the building. After another minute the rain drew a curtain between me and the plant, so I broke into a ragged jog.

I don't know how long it took me to reach the jetty. Weakness was growing up the shafts of my bones as if the toxins in the marsh were filling my body from the ground up. My head was heavy, my brain light. I couldn't keep the jog up for more than a minute at a time. In between I walked, and the further I walked the slower. Finally I was jogging at walking pace and walking at a snail's pace, and watching the dirt track because I couldn't feel it under my feet.

When at last I looked up and The Wash was a bright line in front of me, the steel jetty marching out into it like a bit of municipal architecture running away to sea, I realized I'd made it. Either there'd been no pursuit or Hollis had managed to contain it. For a moment I couldn't remember what came next. Simply getting here had taken all my thinking, all my failing strength.

I was still wrestling with my woolly brain when Gallagher came out of the security hut. He blinked, I blinked. We regarded one another with mutual surprise and misgivings.

He recovered before I did. He leaned forward, sandy brows drawing together, eyes deep with suspicion, and demanded, 'What are you doing here?'

The world has a misleading view of writers. It reads a passage full of passion, relevance and wit and assumes that it took the same five minutes to write that it took to read. People who have not themselves tried to write never guess how many drafts an author will run through, how bad the first few are, how full the waste-paper bin. Most people are terribly disappointed when they meet an author and find that in conversation he can hardly string three words together and never finishes a sentence without revising it at least twice.

I said, 'Er . . .'

Gallagher peered at me through the rain. 'They let you go? *They let you go?*'

I nodded. 'Yes.'

'After everything they told us? They told us the future of the plant depended on rounding you up. All of you, but you especially. And they let you go?' He leaned closer, looking for the mark of Cain. '*Did* they let you go?'

They always say honesty is the best policy. 'No. I opened an upstairs window, jumped out, fought my way past the gatehouse and ran here. What do you think? Of course they let me go.'

176

'Why?'

I breathed heavily at him. 'Because somebody's got to sort this mess out, and the clowns in the boardroom weren't making much headway, so they decided it was my turn. They want me to talk to the guys in the terminal.'

He sniffed. 'We could take them, you know. Any time.'

'Well, maybe you could,' I said. 'And maybe you couldn't. And maybe no one'll ever know whether you did or not, because after the little bits of you have stopped raining down from the sky the question of who took whom will be immaterial. Now, are you going to let me through? Or shall we just wait here together until Costigian gets bored enough to want a smoke?'

You don't get to be head of security at a major industrial complex by being stupid. Gallagher had known what Wilson required of him last time we tried to leave here and he'd done it. He wasn't sure what was expected of him now. He thought if his company secretary had had fresh orders for him, he'd have called him directly, not passed a message via someone who an hour ago was an enemy. But this talk of explosions was making him nervous.

'Just a minute. Just a minute. You're not going anywhere till I've talked to Mr Wilson. Frank,' he called inside, 'come out here and keep your eye on Dr Marsh for a minute while I have a word with Mr Wilson.' Frank came out, Gallagher went inside. But Gallagher was the bright one, so on the whole it was a good trade.

I said, conversationally, 'I'm not telling you this because I like you, right? But if you smell smoke, get on that ATV and drive. Drive as fast as you can and don't stop for anything.'

These men knew what was in the vats. All the time they'd worked here there would have been constant reminders of how catastrophic a moment's carelessness could be. The mere idea that someone might strike a match in there was enough to turn them cold.

'In fact,' I said, 'I've changed my mind. I'm not going out there. It's not my jetty – why should I care if it blows up? Let's get the hell out of here now. I'm only little: you can carry me on the parcel shelf.' I moved towards the swamp-bike.

'Hang on. Hang on.' Frank should immediately have put his hand on my wrist. Instead he half-turned back towards the security hut. 'Joe? She says they're going to blow up the jetty. Joe! Nobody's paying me to get blown up.'

'Me neither,' I said with conviction. 'If Mr Wilson wants that mad Canadian talking down he can talk him down himself! I've had enough of both of them. You don't want me on your jetty? Great – I don't want to be there. Take me back to the plant.'

'Joe. Joe! She says she's going back to the plant, Joe.'

Gallagher was still trying to get through to Wilson. Now he had a mutiny to quell as well. He put the phone down and strode back outside. 'Nobody's going back to the plant . . .'

'I am,' I insisted. 'I'm not walking up half a mile of steel scaffolding with a bomb on the end of it. You can't make me.'

One of them had to say it: it turned out to be Frank. 'Oh yes we can. If that's what Mr Wilson wants, that's what you're going to do.' Large hands propelled me forward, past the hut and on to the jetty. 'It'll be all right. He won't blow it up with you there. You're his friend, he won't blow you up. Give him a shout, let him know you're coming.'

As a professional story-teller I rather felt the scene needed more depth. More resistance, more coercion. I should start weeping hysterically and go on to the jetty only when they threw me on. But I wasn't after the Booker Prize and time was more important than plot integrity. The only ones who had to believe in it were the guards, and they were convinced.

So I went. One of them shouted after me, 'Hurry!' and I broke into that weary, cumbrous jog for the last time. The steel deck vibrated and softly sang beneath me.

By the time I could see the terminal the security hut had dissolved into the rain. I slowed to a walk and raised my voice. 'Marion? Costigian. It's Clio.' The wind hurled the words back in my throat.

I didn't think the terminal would blow up around me. I

178

thought if he'd waited this long he'd wait until he had news, good or bad. Still I was walking on eggshells, every muscle taut, the hairs pricking on the back of my neck. If it happened, it would probably happen too quick for thought, but still I listened for the first soft whoof of flame.

I rounded the corner of the building and found the office door lying wide. 'Marion? Costigan? Are you there?'

The office was empty but for the quiet body of John Tarrant. The door into the shed was open too. The stench of the vats hit me afresh. I called again.

This time Marion replied. I still couldn't see her. I moved in the direction of her voice, my sleeve to my face.

Maybe it was the fumes making my eyes water, maybe it was the shadows inside the shed, but I didn't see them until I was almost close enough to trip over them. They were against the wall where the pipes ended in four great valves. They were sitting on the floor.

At least, Marion was sitting with her back against the wall, her red head resting against the steel plates. Her eyes had followed me from the door and when she saw I'd spotted her she managed a smile. She made no move to get up.

Costigan was also on the floor, sprawled like a sleeping bear, his head in Marion's lap, his eyes shut. His skin had the same jaundiced cast as John's had just before he died. He was unconscious. One arm lay across him, the other trailed on the steel floor, palm up, the fingers curled into a soft fist. His chest lifted in short, shallow breaths that crackled in his throat.

I dropped on my knees beside him, groping for his pulse. When I lifted an eyelid with my thumb the pupil reacted to light, that was all. 'How long has he been like this?'

Marion gave a tiny shrug that would not disturb him. 'Oh, maybe half an hour.' She seemed hardly to know that he was dying; or rather, she knew and hardly seemed to care. She gave a weak chuckle. 'He wanted to know what was in each of the vats – what would burn, what wouldn't. So he took the lids off and went round sniffing them. Damn fool. But he worked out which was the best to use.' She tapped the pipe by her head. There was a trailing rag wadded into the

179

valve. 'This one. Then he started throwing up, and then he passed out.'

Of course, she was dying too. She was still conscious, that was all. There was no strength left in her. If I'd pulled Costigian off her she couldn't have walked out of the shed. The toxins that had been eating away at both of them these last couple of hours had hollowed them out, reduced them to husks. Conscious or unconscious, they were finished.

'Why did you stay in here?' I heard my voice break and didn't care. 'The air's better in the office. Or you could have sat outside on the deck.'

She smiled again, weary and knowing. Her lips were violet with cyanosis. They'd considered that. Of course they had: they'd had a couple of hours to think about it. 'We were afraid we couldn't get back quickly enough if they rushed us. We reckoned if we stayed here there was nothing they could do faster than we could strike some matches.' She rattled the box in her right hand. Her left was stroking Costigian's thick hair, absently, as if he were a pet.

And I didn't know what to do. I'd come to tell Costigian to blow the terminal. Not to wait but to do it now. There was a chance to save four lives that way – George, Jimmy, Hollis and that gentle, useless bloody doctor Donald Rodway. We might kill ourselves in the process but it wasn't inevitable. If we ran like stink and went into the water when the flames came at us, we might make it.

But the situation had changed. However long the fuse, if we blew the terminal my friends were going to die. They couldn't run. They couldn't crawl. I might, given enough time, lug Marion beyond the immediate danger zone, but I'd never get Costigian far enough to make any difference. He would have to stay, and I thought she'd want to stay with him.

I still had a choice. I could leave now. I could go back to Frank and Joe Gallagher. I could slip into the water and see whether I'd reach land or drown first. I could rig some kind of fuse before I went. God forgive me, I could ask Marion to wait five minutes then start Armageddon without me.

I'd no doubt she would do it. That's why they'd stayed

behind. If they'd had second thoughts they'd have left before one of them was sick enough to collapse and the other too sick to help him. They'd had a choice too: between escaping the worst of the fumes and staying where they could finish the job even when they were dying. They wouldn't leave now if I could have moved them. Next time the jetty echoed to the sound of running feet, Marion would set fire to the rag Costigian had forced into the valve.

'How did you know it was me?' I asked. 'I was scared you'd blow the place up before I got within hailing range.'

She smiled thinly. 'As a rule, storm-troopers sound bigger.'

Choices? I had none; or anyway, none that mattered. I could die with my friends here, I could go back to Growth Industries and die with our friends there, I could go into the water and die alone. And I was too damn tired to do anything more.

Marion said, 'What are you doing here anyway?'

What was I supposed to say? There's a chance for the others if you'll burn yourself to death now. Actually, that was exactly what I'd come to say. But finding them like this changed everything. It was always going to be a terrible risk, starting a fire that would blow the terminal halfway to Lowestoft. But there was an outside chance if we ran, if we went over the side, if we dived deep and stayed down until our lungs were bursting while the firestorm raged above us until all the oxygen was consumed and it began to die back.

Now they were helpless and I couldn't go through with it. It wasn't logical. Costigian was already past feeling his flesh sear. Marion would feel it, but the explosion would cut her suffering short. And our people at the plant might still be helped if we acted now – if I told her what I knew. I didn't think Marion's courage would fail the way mine had.

I took a deep breath. 'It's all over. We've won. Wilson's given himself up. There's an ambulance on its way to GI to take care of the others, and a ship's coming here to take us off. Put the matches away. We won't need them now.'

Twenty-One

If there'd been any point, I'd have tried to move them – at least Marion, at least as far as the door, where she could breathe. But there was no point at all. I hoped she too would be unconscious before the tanker arrived.

I wasn't sure what to expect. I doubted the captain would be prepared to ram the jetty with his precious ship, so the cautious Mr Wilson wouldn't ask him to. The surest way would be to plant an explosive device under the terminal and detonate it as the tanker moored. If the ship went up as well there would be no one left to argue the proposition that it had caused the accident.

It seemed a good way for a clever, cautious man to protect his interests, but it was only speculation on my part. Even if I was right, there was nothing I could do to prevent it. There was no radio among the instruments: I looked. All I could do was wait, and hope Marion wouldn't guess what it was I was waiting for.

At intervals I went outside. The fresh air controlled the nausea. The third time I went outside there was a black shape on the horizon that, even as I watched, began to resolve itself into the V-shape of a big ship standing high in the water. An unladen tanker, for instance, approaching head-on.

I shivered. My hands were suddenly ice-cold: I chafed them as I went inside. I tried to speak lightly. 'They're coming now. It'll soon be over.'

She looked at Costigian's blank, blind face in her lap. 'In time for him, do you think?'

'Oh yes,' I said confidently. 'They'll flush his lungs out with oxygen. He'll be fine.'

'I'm glad.' Her voice wasn't much more than a whisper

now. 'He's a good man. A decent man. I was hard on him. I wouldn't like him to die with that between us.'

I knelt quickly and put my arms round her. My throat was full. Only the certainty that when he died and she died I'd die too kept me from crying. I managed, 'He understood. He had a lot of respect for you. He said you were a good cop.'

I felt her slow grin against my cheek. 'That's nearly a proposal in our business, you know.'

Crouched together like that, me holding Marion and Marion holding Costigian, we waited for the ship. I can't say for how long: maybe ten minutes. We couldn't see out from where we were, but towards the end we could hear it manoeuvring – big engines roaring, the churn of propellers, the slap of waves along the hull.

I waited for the soft impact as the big ship, manoeuvred with improbable delicacy by its bow-thrusters, bumped against the great fenders protecting the terminal. If I'd guessed right, that would be about the last thing I knew. If Ernest Wilson was where I expected, sitting in his car with his binoculars focused on the scene and his narrow accountant's finger poised over a radio transmitter, that was when he'd press the button. And thousands of tons of finely engineered steel would erupt under me and through me, and a great chemical fire would shoot up the sky.

Quarter of an inch of steel plate and a few feet of salt air away, the sound of the ship was mounting to a climax, her captain on the bridge and her crew on the hawsers quite unaware that they were making fast for the last time and the next bar they crossed would be the heavenly one. Our time was almost gone. Urgently at the last, afraid of being cut short, I begged Marion: 'If I've done this wrong, forgive me.' And I wasn't sure from the faraway gentleness in her green eyes if she understood or had given up trying to understand. The palm of her hand slipped from Costigian's hair over his closed eyes.

The moment of contact sent a shudder the length of the jetty. I squeezed my eyes shut.

After a couple of minutes I started feeling foolish and opened them again. Nothing had changed. Outside we heard voices raised over the wind and the slap of hawsers. Feet hurried past on the deck and someone was calling my name.

The bright rectangle that was the open door dimmed as people came into the shed. Several of them. People in rubber suits, people in uniforms and respirators, people carrying stretchers and at least one man with a gun. Not a handgun, either – a bloody great assault rifle.

I managed a piping thin greeting of utter banality that seemed the only possible alternative to a wail. 'We're over here.' But there was one thing I felt I ought to make clear. 'There might be a bomb . . .'

The one in front was wearing a respirator, so I couldn't see his face, only that he was a big man in that version of British police uniform that's halfway between SWAT gear and a weekend woolly pully. He came with quick powerful strides, and didn't wait for a stretcher but swung me up in his arms and carried me outside. 'There would have been,' he agreed bleakly, 'but there isn't now. Are you all right?' We were out on the deck by now. He pushed the respirator off his face to see more clearly. 'Good grief . . .'

The wind was still blowing and the rain was still falling, and the tanker lay peaceably to her warps alongside the jetty, and after a while I started to feel human again. Enough to be interested in an explanation.

We owed our lives, after all, to Saul Penny and his boat. At least, to a bit of it.

When the *Keith and Mary* trod him down, Saul had the wit to dive deep and stay under as long as he could. When he had to surface among floating wreckage, breathing without being seen. Only when he heard the trawler complete her victory lap and head off towards Graveleigh did he grab the biggest piece of flotsam he could find and start swimming.

He was in the water for two hours, making a little progress towards Lincolnshire but mostly drifting on the tide. Finally a party of sea-anglers spotted him and pulled him aboard, blue with cold and barely coherent. He had just enough wit to keep them from taking him to The Island. With the mobile signals still blanketed by interference, they headed for the Witham instead.

By the time they landed they'd heard enough to know this was police business; and the local bobbies had more sense than to try to deal with it themselves. The major-incident procedure devised primarily to deal with terrorism swung into action.

The police didn't, at that point, know everything I knew. But they knew enough to realize that, dealing with the Wilsons, they'd need both belt and braces. While their main assault force approached Growth Industries down the marsh road, a support unit was put aboard the tanker. The ship was expected, her appearance would cause no alarm. When she docked, our casualties could be tended on board while the police party secured the terminal.

In the event it didn't go that smoothly. But it was the rough edges that saved all our lives. The tanker was intercepted off Gibraltar Point. Her master knew nothing of what was going on at GI and raised his eyebrows but no objections to taking on a police team. But the boarding took longer than anticipated so that the main unit arrived at GI while the tanker was still three miles out to sea.

Terry Hollis had been removed from the gatehouse by then. But when the police arrived, those who'd locked him up worked out which side their bread was buttered and let him out again, and he made himself known to the police. He didn't know everything but he knew enough to send the police to Ernest Wilson, and to send Wilson to jail.

As an accountant, the company secretary was familiar with percentages. He did some sums now, figured out that hitting the button might cost him another ten years, and told them about the bomb.

Asked what he'd thought he was doing, the diver who planted it looked surprised and said Mr Wilson had given him a stress-monitor to place under the terminal. There'd been some concern as to how the structure was coping with the impact of mooring ships. When it was explained to him what the device actually was, he sat down heavily on the floor with one leg in his wetsuit and one leg out.

I asked about George and Jimmy, and they were safe too, tucked up in the clinic with GI's doctor tending them devotedly. Shivers ran up and down my spine. Clearly Rodway thought he could make up for the fact that he hadn't dared to help us. I wished I could be angry. Instead all I felt was a withering contempt.

Rodway could have prevented much of what had happened, but it had been easier – safer – to shut his eyes to it. The Wilson family would pay for what they'd done, but Rodway would claim he'd done nothing and known nothing and would probably be believed. It wasn't even a lie; but it wasn't the whole truth either. Perhaps he couldn't have saved Nick, but those who'd died since would have lived if this man whose profession was the preservation of life could have brought himself to venture his own. He had John Tarrant's blood on his hands, and Tom Chase's. And maybe Costigian's and Marion's too.

As soon as I could walk I went looking for them. The tanker's second officer took me a way of narrow passages and steep steps to the ship's infirmary. They had been expecting casualties, knew from Saul what we were up against. I found the police surgeon, the ship's medical officer and a medical orderly busy with oxygen masks and hypodermics. With me there too we had more medics on board than people qualified to drive the ship.

The moment I saw her I knew Marion was out of danger. She didn't look great but already she looked better. The oxygen had brought a flush of pink to her skin, and while there were dark smudges on her cheekbones and her eyes were dopey and unfocused under the heavy lids, she no longer had the look of someone marked for death.

The doctors must have thought so too because they'd left her to recover with only an oxygen mask and the orderly for company. Both men were fully occupied with their other patient.

Marion saw me a moment after I saw her and waved me over, propping herself up on her elbows. She pushed the mask down off her face. 'What's happening?'

I told her. 'The Seventh Cavalry got here. Saul's alive – he was picked up by some anglers and raised the alarm. The police are at Growth Industries, and George and Jimmy are OK.'

She looked puzzled. 'But that's what you told me ages ago.'

And of course she was right. It hadn't been true then: fact had followed fiction. In the fullness of time I would have to explain, but for now reassurance would do. I smiled and nodded. 'Marion, everything's OK. It's all over. You're going to be fine.'

'What about the moose?'

From the way they were working at him he was in a lot of trouble. They kept thumping him and listening to his heart and thumping again. His skin was still deeply sallow where they'd bared his chest. Getting oxygen into the lungs doesn't do much good if the heart isn't pumping it round.

One deep voice said sharply, 'He's fibrillating.' And I thought that was it, that he would die before we could get him to a hospital where the miracles of technology would take over the struggle. But I had underestimated the standard of medicine aboard a big modern ship. They had an ECG and they had defibrillators. Big capable hands darted between the unconscious man and the trolley, so quick and deft I wasn't sure which hands were whose.

'Clear.' Costigian's body bucked with the current bolting through him. The wavering line on the ECG went suddenly flat. Then it peaked, just once.

'Again. Clear.'

Marion's hand had crept into mine and I held it tightly. The shock that sent the man's body convulsing upwards had a faint echo in hers. Maybe in mine too.

Again the sharp peak, then the line flattened. Someone said, 'Damn,' in a voice that spoke of defeat.

Someone else said, 'Wait a minute.' We all watched the electric line intently. After the peak came a couple of tiny pulses, mere molehills on the plain. Then there was another peak, up and down like a termites' nest. More of the wavering stuff, then another peak; and after that he settled into a rhythm. Slowly, before our very eyes, his skin changed colour.

The tension eased in the infirmary, the sighs of relief like

187

a breeze in a summer meadow. The ship's MO patted his ECG fondly on its metallic head. 'God bless Mr Faraday.' By then we were all smiling inanely, except for Marion, who had finally let go enough to cry.

I sat with her until she went to sleep, and I was still there a while later when Costigian started waking up. A change in the rhythm of his breathing was the first sign. I looked at him but his eyes were still shut, the muscles of his face lax. I crossed the room for a refill from the coffee percolator, and when I came back his eyes were open. Half-open anyway, heavy-lidded but steady on my face. His lips moved in a whisper. 'Hi.'

'Welcome back,' I said softly.

He remembered what had happened up to the time when he'd passed out, wanted an update from then. I condensed it into a few sentences.

'Saul made it then.' He smiled lazily. 'I'll be damned. Who else?'

'Marion's here – she's fine. She's asleep now but you can talk to her later. George and Jimmy are up at the plant. And Terry Hollis, who actually came through for us in the end.'

'Chase?'

I shook my head. 'No.'

'Do we know that?'

'Yes.'

His face closed for a minute on the pain of regret. Then without opening his eyes he counted them off. 'Nick, John, Tom Chase. I suppose it could have been worse. I thought we were all going to die.'

'Me too.' When he was stronger I'd tell him how close we came.

He opened his eyes then and there was a glint of humour in them. 'Hey, Clio, are you going to write about this?'

Because he was flat on his back in the bunk I could look down my nose at him. 'About this? You think my readers have nothing better to do than read about you?'

His smile slowly broadened. 'You are. Aren't you? I bet you are.'

'No,' I said firmly. 'Of course not. Don't be silly. No.'